BRASSADA HILL

Billy Anders is a killer on the run who is hunted down and fatally wounded by a bullet. His dying wish is to be buried in Brassada Hill where he had grown up, and Jud Brannigan, deputy United States marshal, nods his assent, fully intending to keep this promise.

There's trouble ahead, as some folks keep on hating, believing Billy got what he was entitled to—even Billy's parents disown the body.

Brassada Hill has the usual mix of watering-holes, stores, services and characters. But it has influential people who do pretty much as they like and who instil a sense of awe and fear into the inhabitants of the town.

Brassada Hill is like a powder keg, waiting for a spark to set it off.

Peter B. Germano was born the oldest of six children in New Bedford, Massachusetts. During the Great Depression, he had to go to work before completing high school. It left him with a powerful drive to continue his formal education later in life, finally earning a Master's degree from Loyola University in Los Angeles in 1970. He sold his first Western story to A.A. Wyn's Ace Publishing magazine group when he was twenty years old. In the same issue of *Sure-Fire Western* (1/39) Germano had two stories, one by Peter Germano and the other by **Barry Cord**. He came to prefer the Barry Cord name for his Western fiction. When the Second World War came, he joined the U.S. Marine Corps. Following the war he would be called back to active duty, again as a combat correspondent, during the Korean conflict. In 1948 Germano began publishing a series of Western novels as Barry Cord, notable for their complex plots while the scenes themselves are simply set, with a minimum of description and quick character sketches employed to establish a wide assortment of very different personalities. The pacing, which often seems swift due to the adept use of a parallel plot structure (narrating a story from several different viewpoints), is combined in these novels with atmospheric descriptions of weather and terrain. *Dry Range* (1955), *The Sagebrush Kid* (1954), *The Iron Trail Killers* (1960), and *Trouble in Peaceful Valley* (1968) are among his best Westerns. "The great southwest . . ." Germano wrote in 1982, "this is the country, and these are the people that gripped my imagination . . . and this is what I have been writing about for forty years. And until I die I shall remain the little New England boy who fell in love with the 'West,' and as a man had the opportunity to see it and live in it."

NOA

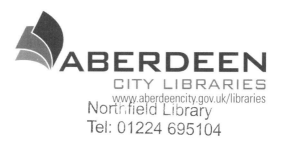

ABERDEEN
CITY LIBRARIES
www.aberdeencity.gov.uk/libraries
Northfield Library
Tel: 01224 695104

Return to ....
or any other Aberdeen City Library
Please return/renew this item by the last day shown. Items may also be renewed
by phone or online

0 5 NOV 2015

BRASSADA HILL

James Kane

GUNSMOKE

This hardback edition 2002
by Chivers Press
by arrangement with
Golden West Literary Agency

ISBN 0 7540 8200 8

British Library Cataloguing in Publication Data available.

Printed and bound in Great Britain by
BOOKCRAFT, Midsomer Norton, Somerset

PROLOGUE

The wind came out of the south, driving shreds of clouds across the sky. It was a high wind that left no sound in the night. On the ground below, it was still; not a bush moved, not a leaf trembled. The air was hot, humid, sticky. It was the kind of Texas night that rasped men's nerves, shortened tempers. It was not the best of times to be traveling.

The riders showed up on the crest of the long dark ridge, singly and in pairs — a dozen hard-faced men, most of them wearing town clothes. They were tired and discouraged. They rode without hurry, without talking, grouping around the big man wearing a badge.

Roger Mason stared bitterly into the night. The badge on his coat gave him the authority to lead the posse, but it was the hate in his heart that drove him.

The horses blew noisily, glad of the respite. The rancid odor of steaming horseflesh stung Mason's nostrils. He shifted slightly, aware of the discouragement among those silent men. It weighed on him, too, making him sour and irritable.

He was younger than most of the men in the posse, not yet twenty-three — big of frame, a bit soft around the middle. Mason was a town man, not a rider, and the long hours in the saddle were a punishment. His back ached from the jolting it had received, but he shut the pain out.

We lost him, he thought, and the realization burned like gall in his throat. He ran the palm of his hand across his beard-stubbled face, wincing a little as he touched the ugly bruises that were just beginning to fade. He was glad that the night hid the look in his eyes, a sharp burning shame as he remembered the battering he had received at the hands of the man they hunted.

Below the ridge a ravine angled off into the darkness. The sound of a rider approaching alerted Mason. He peered down the slope, his hand gripping the stock of his rifle.

"Lee!"

The answering voice eased the tension in him. The riders grouped around Mason relaxed.

The rider was a shadow below them, turning up the slope. The big chestnut he rode blew heavily, tossing his head; bit irons jingled loudly in the stillness.

Mason searched the rider's face as he came up the ridge and pulled to a stop just below him.

"Find anything?" Mason's voice was grim.

Lee Sandino shrugged. He was a lean, wiry man a few years older than Mason. He was a wrangler for the Bar BO, one of the two big ranches in the area, and considered the best tracker in the county.

"Too dark to follow a trail, Mr. Mason." His voice

was respectful as he looked off into the night. "If we make camp here, maybe in the morning—"

"He'll be twenty miles ahead of us by then!" Mason interrupted harshly. He shook his head, a man too full of hate to accept defeat. "We can't let him get away, not after what he did, not this time!"

He turned and challenged the silent men around him. "We'll spread out, keep riding. One of us is bound to come across something—"

Phil Gates, a clerical-looking man with a wispy brown mustache, sighed. "Didn't figure on riding all night, Mr. Mason. My wife—" he glanced apologetically at his companions—"Hetty hasn't been feeling well—"

Mason nodded slowly, fighting his impatience. "I understand, Phil. Sure, go on back."

Gates hesitated. The man next to him, big, burly Lew Stares, said: "Go on, Phil. There's more'n enough of us here to take care of Billy, when we find him."

Gates smiled a bit wanly. The long ride had taken

all the anger out of him.

He said to Mason: "I'll tell your father—"

The rifle shot struck across the night, cutting him off—not too far away, and off to the left. It was followed quickly by two other shots, a signal immediately understood by the tired posse.

"Must be Reed," Lee said. "He and I split a mile down the ravine."

Exultation leaped in Mason's voice. "All right; let's go!"

The riders swept down the ridge behind him. Gates hesitated, undecided. Then, taking a deep breath, he followed.

It took them less than five minutes to converge on the man who had fired the shots.

Reed Ellis, lanky and shaggy-haired, chewing on a cud of tobacco, was holding the bit reins of a saddled, riderless horse. He was in a small clearing ringed by small clumps of live oak.

Mason pulled up alongside him and ran a quick glance over the tired animal. "Billy's horse?"

Reed nodded. "Found him there." He pointed toward the nearest oak clump. "Tied up. Would have missed him if he hadn't whinnied."

Lee Sandino dismounted and examined the horse. "Stone bruise," he said, looking up at Mason. "Ankle's swollen bad." He straightened and looked off into the night. "Billy's afoot, probably not more than twenty minutes ahead of us."

Roger jerked his rifle from his saddle scabbard. "That means he's either looking for a place to hide— or another mount." As Lee nodded slowly, "You know this area, Lee. Where?"

"A half-dozen places to hide, Mr. Mason," Lee answered, "but only one place he can get another horse. The Indian Wells relay station."

Mason nodded. "That's where he's headed, then!" He turned to the others.

"Remember!" he said harshly. "No quarter!"

He settled back in his saddle, his face hard, unforgiving. *"No quarter!"*

— I —

THE UNWANTED

Even the moon looked hot. It was a fat crescent, tilted and smoky red in the western sky—it was a Texas moon. Across its horns thin scuds of clouds whipped by, driven by a wind that stuck a man's shirt to his back. It was a wind that came boiling up out of the Gulf three hundred miles to the south, the vanguard of a tropical storm striking the Texas coast.

Jud Brannigan eyed the moon from the doorway of the Indian Wells Stage Relay Station. He was a rangy man, just turned thirty; a man with an easy stride and an easy smile. But his eyes were light blue, and they could turn chillingly hard. He was an optimist in a land and at a time when this was not always viewed with favor. He was also a lawman, which often added to his difficulties. He wore a Colt .45 on his hip, the holster thonged down and a Winchester repeater snugged in his saddle scabbard, and he was equally adept with either weapon.

The older man in the room behind him said: "Yore steak's ready, Marshal."

Brannigan nodded slightly, but remained in the doorway, looking off. He felt vaguely irritable, troubled by something he couldn't pin down. Somewhere in the night a dog began barking.

"Red moon," Olsen said. "Gonna be trouble before daylight."

He turned and went back inside. Olsen was a long slab of a man, walking crookedly, dragging his left leg. He had been a bronc buster and wrangler in his younger days, but the years had taken their toll. There had been too many bone-jarring rides, too many falls. He considered himself lucky to be working for the Amarillo Stage Line.

Brannigan followed him to the long plank table where his steak and potatoes waited. The station was a long, narrow adobe building set to catch the prevailing winds. A breeze blew through it (when there was a breeze) when the front and back doors were open.

Olsen said: "You stayin' the night?"

Brannigan shook his head.

"What'll I tell them deppities of yores when they show up?"

Brannigan considered this briefly. "Tell them," he said coldly, "I couldn't wait. I'll see them in Brawley. And they better have some damn good reasons for—"

He broke off as somewhere out in the station yard a horse snorted in alarm. The sound came from where Brannigan had left his mount, tied up by the horse trough.

Olsen said: "Sounds like yore cayuse, Marshal."

But Brannigan was already moving toward the door. The horse snorted again, frightened. Brannigan broke into a run, cutting around a small shed. He stopped abruptly, drawing his gun, as he spotted the man trying to mount his big roan, which was shying away from him.

"Damn you!" the man said bitterly. "Keep still—"

Brannigan's cold voice cut across his swearing. "Easy, feller. Move away from that horse!"

The slim figure froze; he was still hanging into the pommel, in the act of mounting. His back was to Brannigan. For a moment the marshal sensed he was ready to defy his order, and he forestalled this by thumbing the hammer of his Colt back. It made an audible, easily recognizable click in the night.

"Turn around," Brannigan ordered. "I want a good look at you."

The man turned slowly, a bitter sigh escaping him. He was young, barely more than a boy, slim and hard and desperately angry. A gun was stuck in the waistband of his trousers, but he kept his hand away from it as he faced Brannigan.

"Yore hoss, mister?"

The lawman nodded, brushing back his coat to give the boy a glimpse of the badge pinned to the inside of his lapel. "Jud Brannigan, deputy United States marshal."

The young man nodded slightly. "Would have to be yore hoss, Marshal. That's the way my luck's been runnin' all my life—"

"If you're looking for transportation," Brannigan cut in coldly, "there's a stage coming through here in the morning."

"I can't wait that long," the boy said. His gaze slanted across the yard. A desperate urgency prodded him into a request he was reluctant to make; he was not the sort to ask a favor of anyone.

"Look, Marshal, it'll just be a loan. As far as Brawley. I'll leave him at Doan's Stables for you."

His voice trailed off as he sensed no concurrence in Brannigan. He shrugged, retreating into a shell of defiance; then, half sneering, he said: "Well, it was worth a try—"

"What are you running from?"

The boy's laughter had an edge to it. "A lot of things, Marshal, a lot of things—"

He studied Brannigan for a moment; then his attention slanted off again, toward the low dark hills beyond the corral, and his slim body stiffened as the sound of riders intruded upon the night.

Brannigan heard it and knew the sound for what it was. He eyed the young man, frowning. "Whatever you did, it'll go easier for you if you turn yourself in."

The boy stared off toward the unseen posse; he did not seem to hear Brannigan.

The marshal's voice sharpened. "You hear me? I promise you'll get a fair trial—"

The youngster swung around, his eyes burning, a mocking smile on his lips.

"Fair trial, Marshal?" He shook his head, his voice sliding off into lost, lonely bitterness. "Not for me, mister—not for Billy Anders—not in Brassada Hill!"

Brannigan took a step forward, something about the young man touching a chord of sympathy in him. *Hell, he had had his own problems with the law once, when he was young and wild . . . .*

"Look," he started to say, "it can't be all that bad." He turned to glance at the oncoming posse, moving toward them at the far end of the small valley, then swung back to Billy.

"Get rid of that gun," he said sharply. "And wait here for me. I'll go talk to them—"

Billy cut him off, his voice harsh now, uncaring. "Some other time, Marshal."

He shoved past Brannigan then, gambling that the marshal wouldn't try to stop him, wouldn't use his gun. He ran recklessly toward the oncoming riders.

Brannigan swung around, his gun targeting the

boy's back. He muttered an irritated curse as he started to run after Billy.

He was a hundred paces behind, trying to spot the running, desperate boy among the shadows by the corral, when the first of the possemen came into sight. He was headed for the relay station and Brannigan when he saw the lawman. He jerked back on his reins, skidding his horse to a stop, and swung his rifle around.

Brannigan had his gun in his hand. He saw the badge glint on Roger Mason's coat, and he yelled: "Wait!" and jerked aside just as the man fired.

The bullet went high and wide, screaming into the night.

From the shadows at the end of the corral, Billy's voice rang sharp and clear. "Here, Mason—over here!"

Mason swung around, fear tightening his face. Brannigan's gaze jerked toward the voice. He saw the boy backed against the pole bars, a gun in his hand. He had the big townman targeted, less than twenty feet away. He saw Roger swing his rifle around. And Brannigan, watching, unable to intervene, saw a confused bitterness run across the boy's face. Then, at the last moment, he jerked his arm up, firing high over Roger's head.

Mason fired back, his bullet driving Billy against the corral posts. He fired once more, deliberately now, sure of his quarry. Billy twisted under the impact of the bullet, his gun slipping from his hand. He turned toward Brannigan as he fell.

The others of the posse came riding up now, falling in beside Mason, rifles ready. Lew Stares said harshly: "It's the kid all right."

Roger rode slowly toward the boy on the ground. Billy was moving blindly, trying to get up. A grim smile twisted Mason's lips. He eased his rifle muzzle down, aiming carefully at the back of Billy's head.

Brannigan swept the rifle muzzle aside and stood astride the dying boy, facing Mason and the grim-faced, tired men behind him.

"That's enough!" Brannigan said coldly. "You stopped him! What more do you want?"

Roger eyed him dispassionately. "Who are you?"

Jud swept his coat lapel back, giving them a

glimpse of his badge. "Brannigan, U.S. marshal!"

Roger slid his rifle back into its scabbard with a deliberate, contemptuous thrust.

"Guess you're right, Marshal. We're through with him."

The boy moaned softly, and Brannigan knelt beside him. Billy was making feeble, clawing motions on the ground. Brannigan raised his head and shoulders, feeling sorry for the boy, and wondering.

"You should have waited," he said softly.

Billy's eyes focused on the lawman's face. He rolled his head slightly, fought to put a smile on his lips.

"Wouldn't have mattered," he said. His voice barely reached Brannigan. "Should have loaned me yore hoss." His fingers dug into Brannigan's arm. "Promise me, Marshal—bury me—Brassada Hill." His eyes brightened, searching Brannigan's face, desperate, appealing. "Only home I know." His voice began to fade. "Promise me—Brassada Hill—?"

Brannigan nodded.

Billy's voice gusted quietly: "Thanks, Marshal." He

closed his eyes and some measure of peace came over his young, bitter face.

Slowly Brannigan eased him down. He came to his feet and eyed the silent riders making a semicircle around him.

"He's dead."

Lew Stares spat on the ground. "Saved us a hanging, Marshal."

Brannigan's gaze settled on Mason. "You could have taken him alive," he said harshly.

Mason shook his head. "You saw it. He took the first shot at me—"

"I saw it!" Brannigan snapped. "He had you dead to rights, twenty feet away — and he shot high. Why?"

"Nerves, maybe," Roger snarled. "Hell, I don't know why he missed — I don't care! And it doesn't matter now, does it?"

He turned to the others. "It's over, boys. Let's go home."

The callousness of these men angered Brannigan. He said sharply: "Where's the sheriff?"

Roger eyed him with truculent impatience. "Home,"

he said shortly. "In bed, sick with pneumonia. Look, Marshal," he went on, "we're legal. Sheriff Breen deputized all of us before we left."

He started to swing his mount around.

Brannigan raised his voice in angry disbelief. "You going to let this boy lie here, just like this?"

Roger minced his horse around, rode up close to Brannigan, glanced indifferently at the body and put his gaze on the marshal. He picked his words, delivering them with cold, unforgiving intensity.

"Here, or anywhere you want to drag him, Marshal!" He gestured toward the dark, silent hills. "Dig a hole out there and dump him in it! Won't be anybody in Brassada Hill who'll care!"

He jerked his mount around and rode off. The others fell in behind him, riding coldly and silently past Brannigan, not looking at Billy's body.

Olsen came up to join Brannigan as the posse faded into the darkness. He glanced down at the body without compassion.

Brannigan turned and eyed him for a moment. Then, softly: "You know him?" He looked down at the boy, lying still by the corral bars.

Olsen nodded. "Billy?" He turned to spit across the body, his eyes flinty, unsympathetic.

"He never was any good, Marshal, from the day he was born!"

— II —
HE BELONGS IN BRASSADA HILL

BRASSADA HILL was a small town on the western edge of the Texas Panhandle, lying just southwest of the old Goodnight-Loving cattle trail, whose broad trace was still visible less than ten miles beyond the town's limits.

Almost a million lean-flanked, half wild steers had come that way since 1865, moving in a steady stream north to the rail towns of Abilene and Dodge City before other closer and more readily accessible shipping points had made the longer drives to Kansas unnecessary.

Small ranches and farms now cut across the old trail, hemming in with barbed wire and posted signs what had once been open rangeland.

Brassada Hill had settled down. It had a stone bank, a meeting hall and a church, and several years of prosperity had brought a smugness to most of the town's citizens, who conveniently chose to forget Brassada Hill's past wildness.

It was midday of the next morning when Marshal Brannigan rode into Brassada Hill with Billy Anders' body draped across the saddle of a lead iron-gray horse. He had wrapped the body in a blanket more out of respect for the boy and decency than in order to hide his identity.

Towering black clouds were riding at his back, blotting out the sun; the feel of imminent rain hung in the close air.

Brannigan searched the building line as he rode. He had not slept well, and he was in a sour frame of mind. His badge was in his pocket, inside his wallet. He wore it on his shirt only when he was on official business. Riding now, he was thinking of his two partners, Joe Sequoia and Jim Granite, who were probably waiting for him in Brawley. He found himself impatient to leave Brassada and ride on before the rains came.

A sign over a saloon drew his attention, the name intriguing him: The French Slipper. It was not one of the common run of names for Texas bars, which ran more to designations such as Longhorn Saloon or variations thereof.

He pulled up briefly to study it, noting that the windows were boarded up and the heavy storm door closed and padlocked. Brannigan frowned. It looked as if someone were jumping the gun on the coming storm—

A man's deep voice asked pleasantly: "You looking for someone, mister?"

Brannigan turned in his saddle. He was aware now that he had stopped by a blacksmith shop. A brawny man with bared muscular arms and a leather apron was watching him, a pair of tongs in his right hand.

Brannigan said shortly, "I'm looking for the undertaker—"

"Sam Hill," the blacksmith replied. "You'll find Sam's Funeral Parlor up the street, across from the Stockman's Bank." He wiped sweat from his brow with his forearm. "If he ain't in, he'll be in Jake's

General Store, playing checkers."

Brannigan started to swing away. The blacksmith pointed toward the blanket-covered body with his tongs.

"Friend of yours?" There was sympathy in his voice.

"No," Brannigan answered curtly.

He rode on, leaving the blacksmith frowning, wondering at Brannigan's lack of friendliness.

Up ahead, a heavily loaded wagon was pulling out of the Mason Freight Line yard. Brannigan turned aside to let the six-horse team swing by. The driver, a pint-sized man with a huge steerhorn mustache, let his gaze drift without much interest over Brannigan and the body behind him. He spat tobacco juice over the near wheel as he turned south out of Brassada Hill for the long haul to San Antonio.

Roger Mason, clipboard in hand, stood in the yard, checking off items on the invoice. The Mason Freight Line was a big outfit; it ran six to ten wagons a week out to various points in and beyond the Panhandle, and it was the main supplier for Brassada Hill and the ranches and farms around. The office fronted the street; it was at the head of a long ell warehouse and stables. In all it took up a sizable portion of the corner of Main Street and Longhorn Avenue.

Finishing his check-listing, he raised his glance, swinging it idly to the tall man riding by. Recognition stiffened him, and then a quick surge of anger brought a scowl to his face . . . .

Behind him a man about his size, but twenty-five years older, emerged from the warehouse and walked to him, his thoughts on business.

"We'll have to do something about that Rawlins shipment, Roger," he began. "This is the third time they've been delinquent in their—"

His voice trailed off as he saw that Roger wasn't listening. He followed the younger man's gaze to Brannigan riding by, and a frown came into his light blue eyes. Frank Mason was about fifty, heavier around the middle and chest than his son, a harder, more solid man whose sense of worth rested on twenty years of successful business operation.

He said, faintly worried: "What is it, son?"

Roger turned, shoved the clipboard into his father's hands and started for the street in long angry strides. Frank started after him, then stopped. His gaze went past Roger to the tall man pulling up in front of Sam's Funeral Parlor, and now the cutting edge of an old fear came to hurt him, bringing an uneasy glitter to his eyes.

Marshal Brannigan dismounted in front of the funeral parlors and eyed the weather-beaten sign above the closed door. A quick splatter of rain came and went, like a scouting party sent out from the great blue-black mass moving out of the south. It brought with it the first faint sense of coolness to Brassada Hill . . . .

He put his hand on the latch and was about to enter when Roger's angry voice said: "Marshal!" He remembered the voice, and he didn't like the man's tone, as he had not liked it the night before. He pulled back and turned slowly to face the big young man striding toward him across the street . . . .

Behind Roger, just coming out of a dress shop, a

girl paused, attracted by the voice. Her gaze darted past Roger to Brannigan and slid to the blanket-covered body on the horse nosing the rail. She was a thin, frail-looking girl of eighteen, but she looked younger; she was not a very pretty girl.

Her gaze rested on the body, and fear brightened her eyes. She shrank back slightly, as though a ghost had come back to haunt her . . .

Brannigan was waiting for Roger, the frown in his eyes held in check. His glance slid past the man to the girl in the doorway, and something elusive about her nagged at him. Then he jerked his attention back as Roger's voice lashed at him with barely concealed fury.

"Maybe you didn't understand me last night, Marshal!" He pointed a finger at Billy's body, his face working with almost fanatical hatred. *"Get him out of here!"*

Brannigan's voice was cold. "Why?"

"Because he doesn't belong in Brassada Hill!" Roger said thickly.

The man's implacable and unreasoning hostility angered Brannigan.

"Where *does* he belong?"

"I don't know," Roger replied. "But not here! Not in Brassada Hill!"

He whirled, striding quickly to the horse burdened by Billy's body, and started to untie the animal—

"Hold it!"

Something in Brannigan's flat, hard voice stopped Mason. He turned slowly to face the marshal as Brannigan stated without compromise: "He stays!"

For a long bitter moment Roger studied the quiet determination in Brannigan's eyes. Then he let some of his boiling anger out in a long sigh.

"I see," he said. His voice was strained. "You taking over, Marshal?"

"I promised Billy a decent burial," Brannigan said. "He's entitled to that much."

Roger turned his gaze to Anders' body. "You're wrong, Marshal. Billy got all he was entitled to last night!"

He paused, eying Brannigan. "You'll never bury him in Brassada Hill, Marshal! I'll see to that!"

He whirled then and went striding back toward the freight office. Brannigan watched him for a moment;

then his gaze went to the girl across the street. But she, too, was hurrying away, following Roger. He shook his head, trying to remember. Then he turned and went inside the funeral parlor.

Frank Mason was waiting for his son in front of the office. He put out an arm, stopping him as Roger was about to walk past him.

"Billy?"

Roger looked back to the funeral parlor and nodded. "I told him," he said thickly. "I told that United States marshal—"

His father cut him off. "Let them be. Billy's dead! He can't hurt anybody now."

Roger eyed him with bitter anger. "No!"

He turned as the frail-looking girl came up. She paused a few feet away. She was a timid girl, with a haunting sadness in her eyes.

"It is Billy, isn't it?"

Her father nodded brusquely. "Go home, Virginia. This doesn't concern you."

She started to move away, paused. Her gaze went to her brother, and a pleading note entered her voice.

"Roger—"

He ignored her, as he usually did. He was still looking toward the funeral parlor, a wild and unreasoning hatred running through him. He swung back to face his father. "I don't care if he is a federal officer, he has no right to bring that body here."

Virginia's voice intruded softly, sadly. "Why not?" There was a faint defiance in her eyes which held as Roger turned his angry gaze on her.

"If Billy Anders belongs anywhere, he belongs in Brassada Hill!"

— III —

"SOME FOLKS KEEP ON HATING"

Marshal Brannigan looked around the empty reception room. It was modestly furnished with a rolltop desk in a corner, a number of straight-backed chairs, several brass spittoons and a long low walnut table on which several old editions of the *San Antonio Gazette* were displayed, along with two or three journals on modern day embalming and undertaking from Chicago.

Standing there, Brannigan had the feeling he was in a doctor's office. There was something efficient and sterile about the place, and a lingering faint odor of carbolic did not dispel the impression.

Old but clean and heavy drapes shrouded a doorway beyond. He called: "Sam," and, when he did not get a response, went into the other room.

It was a little bigger than the reception hall, and it held a number of caskets in tiers along one wall. Brassada Hill was a step away from frontier utilitarianism, Brannigan noticed. There were no plain pine boxes in evidence. Those he saw were better made, shellacked and varnished and satin-lined.

A rather large and ornate casket lay on sawhorses in the middle of the room, the ugliness of the sawhorses camouflaged under yards of soft white cloth. A small bouquet of flowers had been placed on the casket; the lid was closed. It was, Brannigan thought, a place of repose, a place where death, like the reception room behind him, kept a sterile and carbolic distance.

He surveyed the casket in the center of the room for a moment, then walked on to a door which opened into the embalming room. In contrast, this room had a workmanlike appearance, from the freshly scrubbed embalming table, the carbolic-scoured sink, the apron hanging on a hook, to the rubber gloves on the table.

Brannigan withdrew, pausing briefly again by the coffin with the flowers on it. Curiosity tempted him to open the lid, but he felt it would be an invasion of privacy, and he left the room.

Some children had gathered around the blanketed body of Billy Anders when Brannigan stepped outside. He eyed them for a moment, and then a stout, middle-aged woman with a shopping basket on her arm called sharply from across the street: "Timmy, Jamie, come away from there!" And to the gawky, slightly older girl: "You, too, Sandy."

One of the boys said: "Aw, Ma —"

The woman cut across his protests. "You go on home, all of you, before I send for you father!"

They moved away reluctantly.

Brannigan started to untie his horse, then changed his mind. It was only a short walk, he noticed, to the general store up the street. He glanced toward the Mason Freight Line office, but Roger and the girl must have gone inside . . . .

The wind was at ground level now, beginning to

swirl dust in the street. Trees lined the walks, and the branches creaked slightly, bowing to the coming storm. A grayness spred a twilight gloom over Brassada Hill, although it was only midday . . . ,

The lawman felt the weight of curious eyes on him as he walked. He was a stranger with a corpse, and word, he thought, had not yet been spread by Mason that he was also a Federal officer.

The church stood all alone, dominating a small hill at the far end of town. It was a white clapboard building, narrow-fronted and with a steeple thrusting up into the sky. Somehow its New England austerity contrasted sharply with any feeling of open Texas Panhandle hospitality.

Jake Weinberg's General Store was big and well supplied. Kegs of nails, horseshoes and farm implements were lined up on either side of the door, protected from the harsher elements by a wooden awning that overhung the plank walk.

It was not a busy time of day in Jake's. A middle-aged clerk with a stolid Germanic face was waiting on a bib-overalled farmer. Beyond, a buxom woman was idly fingering bolts of silk and gingham.

Brannigan walked up to the clerk. "I'm looking for Sam Hill," he said.

The clerk glanced up at him, then nodded toward a rear door. *"Ja!* In back." His German accent was thick and a bit impatient.

Brannigan went around the counter and pushed aside curtains hanging in a doorway.

A man's thin, excited voice said: "That ain't fair, Sam! You knew I wasn't paying attention —"

"All's fair in love and war and checkers," Sam replied. He was a thin, angular man in his early forties, as sharp-eyed as a ferret, with a neck like a crane. His brown hair was thin on top, shaggy on his neck. He had a perpetual look of sardonic amusement, as though he compensated by facing death in his work with humor.

"Sam Hill?"

Sam looked up from the small table and the checkerboard to the big man framed in the doorway. Across from him Jake Weinberg swung around. He was a hulking sort of man, ears sticking out from a graying head, and the thin, reedy voice seemed strangely incongruous in the man. He was a widower, his children grown and gone, and ambition had gone with them.

"This is a private area, mister," he said, but his tone was not unfriendly. "If you can wait outside a few minutes —"

Sam cut in: "Aw, hell, Jake — the game's over."

He stood up. "I'm the undertaker," he said to Brannigan. "You want to see me on business?"

Brannigan nodded.

"I have a body I want buried."

Sam's eyebrows rose, but he turned and looked at the store owner. "Can't afford to turn away business, not the way things have been lately."

He started out with Brannigan. "Where'd it happen? Out of town?"

Brannigan shrugged.

They went outside and walked back to Sam's place. A small group of townspeople were on the walk, eying the blanket-covered body. They observed the approaching marshal with hostility.

Sam paused, his sharp gaze sliding from the closed

faces on the walk to the body. Some inkling of what he would find under that blanket came to him. He had heard what had happened last night, and now he turned a questioning look to Brannigan.

But Brannigan was striding to the body. He paused and looked back and said levelly: "Give me a hand with him, Sam!"

The undertaker joined him by the body. Someone in the group on the walk said grimly: "You're not burying him here, Sam!" and Brannigan jerked his head around to locate the voice. But all the faces were pinched and hostile, and the man did not repeat himself.

Sam pulled the blanket away to expose Billy's face. He turned to Brannigan, his face stiff.

"Mister —" he began.

"Brannigan!" Jud cut in coldly. He showed Sam his badge. "Marshal Brannigan!"

Sam stood still, shaking his head.

Brannigan said decisively: "We'll take him inside."

They left Billy's body on the embalming table in the

back room and returned to the reception office. Sam settled uneasily in his chair in front of his desk. His face was grave.

"Marshal," he said, "I'll keep the body here for you until you can make other arrangements. But —" he sighed—"I don't think you'll find anyone in Brassada Hill who'll pay for his funeral."

Brannigan was eying the framed diploma on the wall; he turned and put his level gaze on the undertaker.

"Why? He can't hurt anybody now."

Sam considered this for a long moment. His gaze was guarded, his features remote. He did not want to get involved in this.

Brannigan said, frowning: "Why, Sam?"

Sam shrugged. "Alive or dead," he said slowly, "some folks keep on hating."

"Mason?"

The undertaker gestured toward the window. "Like maybe most of the people in this town, Marshal."

He started to turn back to the paper work on his desk. He thumbed through it, his manner negative, slightly unfriendly.

"I'm sorry, Marshal."

Brannigan frowned. "What did the boy do, any-way?"

Sam Hill swung around; he eyed Brannigan with faint distaste.

"Killed the woman he was working for—Cynthia Choquette." His voice turned sour. "Used a shotgun on her, at close quarters." He glanced toward the room beyond the curtains. "Her body's in that casket inside; she'll be buried Saturday."

"Anyone see him shoot her?" Brannigan's voice was short; the town and the people in it grated on him.

Sam Hill gave him a long look, then turned back to the papers on his desk. It was evident he did not con-sider the question worth answering.

The marshal crossed to him, anger burning like a fuse inside him. He put a hand on the undertaker's thin shoulder and jerked him around.

"It's a fair question!" he snapped. "Who saw it?"

Sam Hill's face turned sullen. "Nobody saw it, far as I know."

Brannigan's look burned contemptuously into him; Sam reacted with a faint show of defiance.

"Look, Marshal, it doesn't matter that no one saw him kill her. But a lot of folks saw him come running out of the alley behind The French Slipper. You passed in front of it if you came in from the south."

Brannigan nodded slightly, and Sam continued: "That's where Billy worked. He was carrying the shotgun that killed her. He dropped it stealing the horse he rode out of town."

Brannigan stared at the mortician for a long time. "Let me get this straight, Sam. Billy Anders stole a horse and ran—and that was enough to convict him in the eyes of ·this town?"

Sam Hill answered harshly: "Far as the people in Brassada Hill go, yes!"

He shook his head, his gaze going to the drapes hiding the rooms beyond. "I guess you'd have to know the boy, Marshal. He was born with a chip on his shoulder a mile high. One time or another he's had trouble with everyone in and out of Brassada Hill."

Brannigan's gaze followed Sam's. He was remembering the boy he had stopped from taking his horse— the pinched face, the defiant pleading that had turned almost immediately to a fatalistic acceptance of his lot. In a small way Brannigan felt responsible for the boy's death.

He let out a long slow breath. "What about his folks? Will they bury him?"

"The Anders?" Sam Hill's smile had a knife edge to it. "Well, you might try them. They run a boarding house on Foster Street — just around the corner from the bank."

Brannigan headed for the door.

Sam Hill said after him: "But you'll be wasting your time, Marshal." As Brannigan paused, "No one in this town is going to lift a finger for Billy, alive or dead!"

Brannigan gave him a long cold look.

"You're wrong, Sam," he said levelly. "Someone is."

He slammed the door behind him as he went out.

— IV —

"WHEN DID YOU BECOME A MAN, SON?"

FRANK MASON came out of the warehouse into his office and paused beside Charley Springer, his bookkeeper, bending over a ledger on a slant-top table. A small worry was gnawing at Frank's nerves.

"See Roger anywhere, Charley?"

Charley paused, pushing his green eyeshade up on his pink forehead. He was a thin, dry man with wisps of white hair. He looked like a man who'd break in two in a strong wind.

"Headed up the street," Charley said. "Said he needed a drink."

He paused, eying Frank. "Never saw him act like this before, Mr. Mason. Kind of like this whole thing was personal."

Frank nodded, his voice distracted. "Guess it's more than the beating, Charley." He glanced toward the street, his lips tightening. "That Rawlins shipment should be coming in at any time. Don't let them unload. I want to talk to the driver —"

Charley said: "When will you be back?" But Frank was already going out, and he didn't answer. Charley shook his head as he turned back to the ledger.

Frank walked swiftly past the bank, nodding to a few people who greeted him. He saw Brannigan ride by, and he paused to watch the marshal turn down Foster Street.

The worry in him turned into a worm of fear; he felt a dark chill spread through him. The big lawman was like a nemesis, opening dark and long closed doors.

He walked past the boarded-up and silent French Slipper and averted his gaze; farther on was the Longhorn Bar, now the only saloon in town.

Roger was at the bar, a glass of whiskey being poured for him by Kenyon, the bartender. It was not the first drink his son had had, Frank noticed, and anger showed in his eyes.

He reached Roger just as his son was starting to lift the glass to his lips and clamped his fingers on Roger's wrists. He glanced angrily at the bartender, and Kenyon shrugged and moved away.

Frank said roughly: "Since when have you started drinking in the middle of the day, son?"

Roger pulled his father's hand away from his wrist. His eyes were dark, burning with an unspeakable hatred.

"When I became a man — two days ago!"

He started to lift the glass again, paused. "Or don't you think I'm old enough, Pa?"

Frank reacted to the hostility in his son's voice. "You're old enough," he said harshly. "All I'm asking is why."

Roger's lips curled. He flipped the glass to his lips and downed the fiery whiskey in one gulp. He didn't even gasp. Roger was a man drinking because of hate, not pleasure.

Frank's face showed a mixture of confused anger and concern.

"What the devil's gotten into you lately, ever since

you had that trouble with the Anders' boy?" He went on grimly as Roger's eyes met his with cold anger. "All right. Billy handed you a beating. Thirty pounds lighter and four inches shorter." He shook his head. "Your pride was hurt. I can understand that. But it's over and done with, son!"

"Is it?" Roger's voice was thick and ugly.

He turned and reached for the bottle and started to pour himself another drink. Frank batted the bottle out of his hand; it crashed to the floor behind the bar.

"Leave that damned stuff alone!"

Roger turned slowly to face him; his eyes searched his father's angry face as though looking for an answer to his own inner turmoil.

Kenyon came up, his manner that of a man wanting to be of service. Frank waved him away.

"That hardware shipment from Rawlins," he said harshly, "you're the one who's been handling it. It's coming in now." He put a hand on his son's shoulder. "Come on; let's get out of here."

Roger shook his head. He turned to the bartender, who was sweeping up pieces of glass behind the bar and dumping them into a container.

"Another bottle, Kenyon."

The bartender nodded, but he glanced at Frank first; the Masons ran Brassada Hill.

Roger reacted to the look, his voice turning ugly "A bottle, Kenyon! I'm old enough!"

Kenyon shrugged. He reached behind him for a bottle of whiskey, set it on the bar in front of Roger and moved away.

Frank glared at his son, anger thickening his voice.

"You drinking to prove to me you're a man? Or—" as Roger sneered—"because that United States marshal brought Billy Anders' body back to town?"

Roger picked up the bottle, turned away from his father and started to pour himself a drink.

Frank reacted to the silent snub; he clamped his fingers on his son's shoulder and jerked him around.

"Damn you — *answer me!*"

Roger eyed him with implacable decision. "I want Billy Anders out of Brassada Hill!"

Frank shook his head, not comprehending. "Why?" He searched his son's bitter, closed face for an answer to his unreasoning hatred.

"The boy's dead. Whatever differences you had

with him, they're over and done with!" His tone softened and took on a more conciliatory note. "Why stir up needless trouble, Roger? Let that marshal bury him wherever he wants —"

Roger's voice cut him off with one explosive word: *"No!"*

Frank stared at him, speechless before the dark, crawling fury in his son's face.

"I won't have Billy Anders buried in the church cemetery beside my mother! I won't have him contaminating the ground she lies in! Don't you understand? I won't have him in Brassada Hill!"

Frank's voice was shocked. "Roger!"

Roger's gaze burned into his; dark, compelling. "She was my mother, wasn't she?" He grabbed Frank's shoulders and shook him, his voice tortured. *"Wasn't she?"*

Frank's face was a stony mask. "Why do you ask?"

Roger dropped his hands by his sides.

"You stood beside me at your mother's funeral," Frank said bleakly, "when we buried her, three years ago this Saturday."

Roger nodded slowly. It was what he wanted to

hear; but the doubt in him did not leave, nor his torment. He turned back to his glass and poured himself a drink.

Frank eyed him for a long moment, knowing further words were useless. His shoulders slumped as he turned and went out.

— V —
"MAY HE BURN IN HELL—"

The first hard splatters of rain began to whip into Brannigan's face as he turned down Foster Street and started looking for the Anders boarding house. The wind moaned against the wooden buildings, rattling loose windows. It was almost gloomy there in the narrow street, and Brannigan sensed there would be a bad blow before the day was over.

The Anders boarding house was a two-story frame building, narrow, wedged in between other houses. The wooden sign above the stoop needed painting.

Brannigan tied his horse to the iron hitching post and went inside, moving from the entry hallway to glance inside a front room whose furniture looked stiff, clean and unused.

He heard someone in the kitchen and walked down the hallway, past steep wooden steps climbing to the upstairs rooms, and looked inside at a woman on her hands and knees, scrubbing the kitchen floor. Wisps of iron-gray hair straggled down past pinched, wasted features.

Brannigan said: "Mrs. Anders?"

She turned her head and eyed him, nodding slowly. "I'm full up," she said. She had a tired voice. There was a pail of soapy water beside her. She got to her feet and wiped her reddened hands on her gray apron.

The lawman said: "I'm not looking for a room. I want to talk to you."

She stared at him uncomfortably; this was a woman in whom the juices of life had been sucked dry.

"You a salesman?"

He took his wallet out and showed her his badge. "United States marshal, ma'am — Judson Brannigan."

Fear flickered uneasily in her washed-out gray eyes. She said: "If it's about Billy —"

The back door opened, and Joshua Anders, a

gaunt, gallused man with the stamp of Calvinist New England on his harsh features, entered. He was carrying an armload of wood for the big range against the back wall.

"Looks like it's gonna be a bad one, Lucy —" he said, and then stopped as he saw Brannigan.

Lucy Anders said: "A United States marshal, Joshua. He wants to talk to us."

Joshua walked to the wood box behind the kitchen stove and deposited his armload.

"What about?"

"Your son," Brannigan answered. "Billy Anders."

The man's eyes widened in surprise. "Billy? He's dead." He shot a look at his wife, his brow furrowing. "At least that's what we heard."

Brannigan nodded. "His body's at the undertaker's."

Lucy wiped her hands again on her apron. She looked at her husband, a dark, nameless anxiety in her face. Joshua turned away from Brannigan and picked up his pipe lying on the range shelf, just above the warming oven. His face was cold and uncaring as he thumbed tobacco into the blackened bowl.

"I brought him in," Brannigan went on. "I guess it's up to you to see he is properly buried."

"Bury him?" Joshua whirled around to face the lawman, his voice harsh, cold as granite. "We don't even want to see him!"

Brannigan scowled. "He's your son —"

Joshua didn't answer. He scraped a match on the side of the stove and lighted his pipe.

Lucy said tremblingly: "You came here, expecting *us* to pay for his funeral?"

"Parents usually do," Brannigan said grimly. He eyed them, wondering how Billy Anders had lived there, how any boy could have lived there.

"He *was* your son, wasn't he?"

Lucy shook her head. "We raised him, Marshal. But he wasn't ours —"

Brannigan looked at her for a moment, then turned his attention to Joshua. The indifference of these people angered him.

"What kind of parents are you?" he snapped. "Billy's body is lying on a table in Sam Hill's back room —"

Joshua gave him a contemptuous look. "Let him lie

there, mister! He's no concern of ours!"

Brannigan stared at the man. "Why? Because this town branded him a killer?"

"He killed that woman," Lucy said. Her voice was as dry as tinder; there was no feeling in it.

Brannigan said grimly: "That's what I heard. But how do you know it's true, that he shot her?"

Joshua shook his head. "They say he did it."

"And that's enough for you?"

Joshua's eyes met Brannigan's — pale blue, as hard as glass. "You don't understand, mister. Billy wasn't ours. He was left on the church steps nineteen years ago, when he was less than a year old." He glanced at his wife, but she was looking down at the floor, her hands fumbling aimlessly in her apron.

"We never knew his real ma and pa. Itinerants, probably, passing through town."

Lucy looked up now, her voice thin. In it was a justification she had forced herself to make for all those years. "We took him in, tried to make a good home for him. But he was born mean, that boy—mean and hating —"

Brannigan looked at her, quiet anger in his eyes.

"But he lived here then?"

Joshua nodded. "Until he went to stay at that —" Joshua paused, his eyes cold and condemning — "that woman's house!"

"What house?"

"Place where he worked. The French Slipper, they call it." Then, with strait-laced, unforgiving harshness: "Fancy name — fancy women —"

He crossed to his wife and stood beside her, facing Brannigan.

"Sorry, Marshal," he said stiffly. "We can't help you. You'll have to find someone else to bury Billy."

Brannigan eyed them with barely veiled contempt. He reached in his pocket, took out a small pouch and dumped its contents out on the kitchen table.

"This is all Billy had on him when he was killed last night."

The Anders stared at the items scattered on the table: a small sack of tobacco, cigaret papers, a few coins, a jackknife, and a creased, faded picture of a thin, not very attractive girl.

"I heard your son had no friends in Brassada Hill," Brannigan said. "But he must have had one." He pushed the picture toward them.

"Who is she?"

Joshua shook his head, his lips tightening, a cold and wary look in his eyes.

"We don't want trouble, Marshal —"

Brannigan broke in, his voice hard, grating with impatience: "I'll handle the trouble, Mr. Anders!"

Lucy turned to her husband. "Tell him, Joshua —"

Joshua remained silent. Lucy turned slowly to the lawman. "I don't care if we do get into trouble, Marshal! That's Virginia Mason, Roger Mason's sister!" Thin scorn charged her voice. "You want somebody to pay for Billy's funeral, Marshal — you go see her!"

Brannigan studied the thin, pinched face, alive for the moment with some flickering hate. He turned to Joshua, whose granite features remained closed, unforgiving.

"I'll keep the picture," he said quietly. "The rest of the things are yours."

He walked to the door, where he looked back at them.

"Nineteen years," he said. "Guess they didn't

mean a thing to you, did they, Mrs. Anders?"

A lost and bitter look flared up in the woman's eyes, and she turned away.

Joshua said harshly: "He was no good, Marshal! May Billy burn in hell for what he did!"

ʲ

— VI —
"I'LL KEEP HIM UNTIL TOMORROW"

The wind had a wild, angry sound to it now, scurrying down the alleys and byways of Brassada Hill. The rain came and went in a splatter of big drops, making craters in the dust. The black clouds hurrying overhead were scouts for the bigger storm behind, boiling up behind them.

Here and there along Brassada Hill's main street shopkeepers began to shutter their windows, preparing for the blow.

Marshal Brannigan left his two horses in the stables behind the Stockman's Hotel and made his way east of town to where small frame houses made a pattern under towering chestnut trees.

The sign on the gate said: "Breen," and he pushed it open and knocked on the front door.

A woman opened it, fortyish, pretty; she looked tired, sleepless and worried.

"Brannigan," he said. "United States marshal. I'd like to see the sheriff."

She hesitated.

"I heard he was sick," Brannigan said, "and I won't bother him if it's serious, ma'am. But if he's up to seeing visitors — "

She sighed. "He is," she replied. "I'd rather not, however, unless it's important."

"Quite important," Brannigan assured her, and followed her inside the house. She led him down an entry hall and into a bedroom beyond.

Sheriff Floyd Breen was a florid-faced, hearty-looking man, more politician than lawman, but fair-minded and efficient. He hadn't been sick enough to take to his bed in twenty years, and he took this illness hard. He was recovering, but the spell in bed had taken more out of him than he wanted to admit, and there was a restless look in his eyes as he turned to Brannigan.

His wife said: "Mr. Brannigan, a United States marshal, Floyd. He wants to see you. I told him only a few minutes."

The sheriff waved Brannigan to a chair. "Federal business, Marshal?"

Brannigan shrugged. "Might be." He looked at Mrs. Breen, and the sheriff said: "Leave us, Martha."

She was a woman used to taking orders; she turned and closed the door behind her.

Brannigan said bluntly: "I've got a dead man on my hands, Sheriff. I want to see him buried here."

Sheriff Breen hitched himself up on his pillows. It seemed to take a lot of effort to do so.

"I don't see why you would want to come to me," he began. And then, frowning: "Who is he, Marshal?"

"Billy Anders." Brannigan shrugged. "There seems to be some opposition to having him buried here." The marshal studied Breen. "Not even his foster parents seem to care what happens to the body."

Breen's gaze slid away from Brannigan; he looked down at his hands on the covers. "Can't say that I blame them, Marshal. Billy gave the town a lot of trouble. I ran him out of Brassada Hill once, but he came back. I don't know why he stayed."

"He wanted to be buried here," Brannigan said. "He must have had a reason."

The sheriff sighed. "Maybe. I never found out. But he was mean. I picked him up a number of times for fighting, stealing. I could have sent him to a reform school. I guess I should have, except that I never knew anyone to come out of a place like that any better."

He was silent awhile; then he looked up at Brannigan, a frown in his eyes. "Why are you here?"

Brannigan looked toward the window, where the rain was beginning to slap against the panes. He considered for a moment. "I made him a promise, Sheriff, before he died. I promised him he'd be buried in Brassada Hill."

Breen shook his head not unsympathetically. "Not if the Masons don't want him here," he said. "Try some place else, Marshal."

"I heard the Masons run Brassada Hill," Brannigan said coldly. "I didn't know they owned you, too, Sheriff."

Breen's face stiffened. "There's nothing I can do,"

he said harshly. "And if you must know, there's nothing I want to do—not for Billy Anders!"

Brannigan eyed the lawman for a long moment, feeling frustration. He said angrily: "Billy didn't even get a trial, Sheriff. Call that justice? The jury was stacked against him from the beginning. You deputized a man who hated him, and that posse had him guilty before they even went after him!"

Breen said bitterly: "You don't know this town, Marshal. They would have killed him, with or without a badge behind them."

He slipped down from his pillow, small beads of sweat beginning to glisten on his forehead. "I told them to bring Billy in alive, if they could." He shrugged, his voice fading. "It was the only thing I could do, Marshal."

Brannigan nodded, understanding the man in bed now. He was sick, tired, probably beholden to the Masons for his job. A sheriff was an elected official in most parts of the country, and he depended on votes to keep his position. And most of the votes were the result of influential men—men such as the Masons in Brassada Hill.

He said: "Sorry I bothered you, Sheriff," and turned to leave.

Breen said bitterly: "You don't owe Billy anything, Brannigan. Take him away from here. Bury him some place else!"

Brannigan's smile was cold. "I'll think it over," he said, and went out.

The storm battered Brassada Hill that night, a howling wind-driven rain beating against the cowering buildings, turning the streets into muddy bogs, forcing everyone indoors.

Brannigan, his slicker buttoned up tightly and his hat pulled down over his eyes, fought his way to the funeral parlor and looked in on Sam Hill. The man was just about to close up.

Billy Anders' body was still in the back room, covered by a sheet. There was no one paying respects to the woman lying cold and anonymous in the ornate casket.

Brannigan eyed the coffin, something puzzling him. This was the woman Billy was said to have killed. Yet both lay there in lonely isolation.

"Didn't she have any friends?"

Sam shrugged. "Cynthia Choquette ran The French Slipper like a New Orleans bordello," he said. "But she was discreet about it. The bar downstairs served the best liquor anywhere, and for reasonable prices. She did not flaunt her girls. They remained, for the most part, upstairs and out of sight. But those who wanted that kind of accommodation knew where to go."

"A madam," Brannigan mused. He listened to the rain beat against the building for a moment. "And Billy Anders worked for her?"

Sam Hill nodded. "She must have been a beautiful woman once; there wasn't much of that left when she came to Brassada Hill, a little more than six months ago. Why she came here no one knows. She kept to herself, mostly." He shrugged. "Of course, she wasn't exactly welcomed into Brassada Hill's social circle. But no one complained, either. As I said, she was quite discreet —"

Brannigan said: "She must have had one friend, Sam. The flowers on her casket—who left them?"

Sam Hill took his time answering. He put on his

coat, and Brannigan asked harshly: "Who, Sam?"

"Virginia Mason," the undertaker said. He said it reluctantly.

"Roger Mason's sister?"

Sam nodded. Brannigan looked toward the back room. Sam said slowly, "I don't know why, Marshal. She's a shy girl, not very pretty. I can't even believe she knew Cynthia Choquette."

He walked to the front door, pausing as Brannigan joined him. "I'll keep Billy here until the storm blows over, Marshal. But I won't be responsible for him after —"

Brannigan said: "Someone threaten you, Sam?"

Sam didn't answer, but Brannigan knew that someone had.

He said coldly: "You keep him here, Sam! I'll be responsible!"

The rain slammed into him as he stepped outside. Overhead, the wild and howling wind sang its angry dirge.

But inside, where murdered and murderer lay, it was quiet; the actions of both were now beyond recall.

— VII —
VIRGINIA MASON

Frank Mason was waiting for his son when Kenyon brought Roger home. The rain slashed across the front steps, whipping past Frank into the hallway as he opened the door.

Kenyon, his face wet and strained in the pale lamplight spilling onto the stoop, said: "Sorry, Mister Mason. But he wouldn't leave. I closed up early so's I could get him home."

Frank nodded brusquely. "Thanks, Kenyon." He took hold of his son, who sagged drunkenly against the bartender. "I'll settle the bill with you in the morning," he told Kenyon, and the bartender shrugged.

"No hurry, Mister Mason. Hope he's all right. He drank an awful lot —"

Frank said coldly: "I'll see you in the morning!" When Kenyon stepped back, he hauled his son inside the house and closed the door.

Virginia showed up behind him, pale and self-effacing. He said harshly: "Get some black coffee!" and half carrying Roger, he went into the large, comfortable living room with him and dumped him into a stuffed chair by the fireplace.

Roger stirred; he looked around, his eyes unfocused. "Billy!" he said wildly. "Damn you, Billy —"

The flames from the logs burning in the fireplace played over his slack face. He tried to get up, and his father shoved him back into the chair.

"Made a fool of yourself tonight, didn't you?" Frank rasped, but there was helplessness in his tone and the shadow of a forgotten dread. "First time you drink, and you have to try to drink the place dry!"

Roger lifted his bloodshot eyes to his father. "I killed him," he said thickly. "Why didn't Billy stay there out in the hills, where he belongs?"

Frank said harshly: "You're making too much of it.

Why don't you leave the boy alone?"

Roger started to get up again. "Can't," he said bitterly. "Can't forget . . . "

He fell back into the chair and stared dazedly into the fire. The heat was beginning to steam his wet coat.

"You're soaked," his father said. "I'll get you to your room."

He turned as Virginia came into the living room with a cup of coffee in a saucer. She came up silently to stand by her brother, looking down at him but not really seeing him; looking back to some place else, a private place of her own.

"Hot coffee," Frank growled. "Drink it; it'll clear some of the cobwebs from your head —"

Roger turned and looked at his sister. A bleak hatred twisted his face as he struck out at her. His hand knocked the coffee cup to the floor, the scalding liquid burning the back of her hand.

She jerked back, clutching her burned hand, but she made no sound. Frank said roughly: "What's gotten into you, Roger?" But there was anxiety in his voice; he paid no attention to the girl standing beside him, the pain in her eyes bringing tears.

Roger said: "Ask her, Pa," and tried to get up. But the heat from the fireplace was beginning to get to him. He turned pale, sweat breaking out on his face. He lurched to his feet.

"I think I'm going to be sick," he said and staggered toward the door. His father watched him go out into the rain; then he whirled on his daughter.

"Clean up this mess," he said angrily. "I'll talk to you later!"

He followed Roger outside.

Virginia's tear-shining eyes were remote. She picked up the cup and saucer and went into the kitchen with them. The back of her right hand was a lobster red. She spread a thin layer of grease over it and then went up to her room.

It was a girl's room, painted a pale pink, with ruffles and doodads belonging to younger years. A framed picture of her mother was on her dresser, next to a music box on which a delicate china ballet dancer with a bare wisp of tutu stood poised, ready to dance.

She went to the music box and wound it, and as the tinkling of a Strauss Waltz drifted through the room she went to the window and looked out into the night. She listened to the rain for a long time, lost in another time, a more pleasant place . . . .

Frank Mason came up to her room a half-hour later. He knocked stiffly, and when she answered he came inside and stood by the door, looking around like a man who had not come into the room in a long time and who hardly knew his daughter.

He said quietly: "I've put Roger to bed," and when she didn't answer, he looked closely at her, frowning. She was a tall girl, pale of face, with small freckles around her nose. Her ash blonde hair was pulled tight in a bun on her neck, and she wore clothes that did little for her not very shapely figure.

He seemed to see her for the first time—the way she stood there and waited for him to speak. She never ventured anything herself. She had lived in that house since she was born, and he hardly knew her.

He said with some attempt at gentleness: "How's your hand?"

"It's all right," she said.

"I don't know what's gotten into Roger," he said uncomfortably. She let silence prolong between them, and after a while he walked closer to the dresser and eyed the woman looking out at him from the silver frame. The storm beat against the house, shaking it, and a chill crept into the room.

He wheeled abruptly and eyed his daughter. "Do you know?"

Virginia didn't move. She was looking into the darkness outside, and only after a moment did she shrug.

He said roughly: "There was some talk about you and Billy."

She turned slowly now, her face thin, closed. That face had been closed to him, Frank remembered, for a long time now—from the day Virginia's mother had died.

"Was it—just talk?"

"Just talk," she said. Her voice was a monotone. She was like a parrot, repeating after him, and he felt a frustration rise in him.

"Damn you," he said, "if you're lying to me —"

"Not lying," she said in that strange, uncaring voice. Then, remotely, "Billy's dead. I don't know why Roger is upset."

"Neither do I," Frank said. But the thought weighed heavily upon him. "It can't be the licking Billy gave him."

A flicker of a smile hovered around Virginia's lips. "No," she said. "It can't be."

He looked at her, wanting to strike out at her, to get past her shield of indifference. He felt trapped in a darkness he could not penetrate. But farther back, behind his anger and his frustration, an old fear raised its head, and he said: "No, it can't be—Roger doesn't know—"

Virginia said: "What doesn't he know, Father?"

His face went hard, and his eyes had a sudden guarded look. "Nothing!" He strode to the door, looked back. "Go to bed!" he said. It was an order.

The girl stood by her bed after he left, listening to the storm outside. The smile remained on her lips, like a ghost from happier times.

She said softly: "Billy," and her eyes searched the room like a little girl playing hide and seek with someone.

She went to the window finally and tried to look

out, but the rain made small rivulets down the pane, and she saw only her reflection in it.

She stayed there, listening to the fury of the storm that had come boiling up out of the Gulf of Mexico more than two hundred miles away . . . .

— VIII —
"WE'VE COME TO ATTEND A FUNERAL"

The brunt of the storm passed over Brassada Hill during the night; by early morning the rain had diminished to a gray drizzle. Life began to stir again as horses and wagons churned through the muddy street and shopkeepers took down protective shutters from their store windows.

Few people paid any attention to the two men who rode into town. They came in from the south, riding the tail end of the storm. They rode hunched in their slickers, hats pulled low over cold and alert eyes. They did not look pleased to be there.

Marshal Jim Granite glanced at his partner, Joe Sequoia. "He better be here," Jim said sourly, and

Joe grinned. "That's what that station agent said, Jim."

Jim Granite was a tall, gaunt man nudging fifty; he had a mountain man's sinewy, powerful frame and sharp blue eyes. The brown steerhorn mustache under his nose was generously sprinkled with gray. He wore a Smith & Wesson .44 in a holster on his right thigh, but he was a better shot with the rifle snugged in the scabbard under his right leg. He wore his badge pinned to his coat, but it was hidden now under his slicker. Behind the big chestnut horse he rode trailed a smaller pony, carrying a pack.

His companion was wiry, well built and about twenty years younger. Joe Sequoia was a Cherokee whose father had been part white, and although he had had more schooling than most frontier people, he was seldom given more recognition than being called "that damned Indian!" Joe knew he was accepted in many places only because he carried the badge and the authority of the United States marshal's office. When that failed, he had the ability to make it stick behind a fast gun hand.

With Brannigan, these two men upheld Federal law

over a wide area of the Southwest. There was an easiness between them based on mutual respect. Jud Brannigan was their boss, but each man was his own individual. They had their differences and could be stubborn about their opinions, but when the chips were down they pulled together.

They rode into Brassada Hill, tired, wet and angry at Brannigan. They had a job to do closer to the Mexican Border, and they were not relishing this side trip to Brassada Hill.

It was mid-morning, gray and windy, and the mud in the street was ankle-deep. They turned in toward a low red brick building with a sign nailed over the door: "Sheriff, Concho County." But they found the place locked, and pounding on the door brought no response.

They stopped a man hurrying by, and Jim Granite said: "Federal officers, mister. We're looking for Marshal Brannigan —"

But the man shook his head and went on by, and Jim stared angrily after him. "Not a very hospitable town," he growled, and Joe Sequoia grinned faintly.

"What did you expect, Jim — a brass band?"

They rode on up the street, Jim's slicker open now, his badge glittering wetly. They were met by hostile stares. Passing by the Mason Freight Line, Jim saw a young, heavy-bodied man watching from the warehouse doorway. The man caught the glitter of Jim's badge and turned abruptly, back into the warehouse.

Jim glanced at Joe. "Looks like we're about as welcome in this town as an invasion of polecats," he said sourly.

Joe was eying the building line. "Jud's here somewhere. We could try the funeral parlor."

"I like the saloon better," Granite cut in. "A bartender always knows what's going on in town. And I can stand a snort or two to chase away the chill."

Joe nodded agreement, and they turned in at the Longhorn Bar . . . .

Charley, the Mason bookkeeper, was bent over a ledger, his thin shoulders bowed, a green eyeshade casting a sickly light across his face.

He turned as Roger strode inside, slamming the door behind him. He eyed the young man with nervous apprehension, sensing the violence surfacing in

Roger Mason.

Roger went quickly to the old roll top desk by the window, yanked open a bottom drawer and reached inside for a gun. The .38 Remington was new, unfired. He broke open a box of shells and started to load the pistol.

Coming in from the warehouse, Frank Mason saw his son at the desk; alarmed, he crossed quickly to his side.

"Have you gone crazy?" His voice was harsh. "Put that gun away!"

Roger whirled and jerked his thumb toward the window. "Crazy, eh? Take a look out there!"

Frank turned his attention to the street. Two men were coming out of the saloon—strangers to Brassada Hill and to Frank Mason. They mounted and rode on toward the hotel . . . .

Roger's voice was bitter. "Federal officers, Pa!"

Frank turned to face his son, a flicker of fear crossing his face. He tried to take the gun away from Roger, but his son pushed him away.

Frank said hoarsely: "My God, son — that gun won't help —"

Roger ignored him. He shoved the gun into his coat pocket and went to the door. His father followed him.

"Wait! Don't do anything foolish! Let me talk to them first! Maybe I can —"

"Sure," Roger sneered. "Sure — you talk to them, Pa!" He yanked the front door open and went out.

Frank stood there, indecisive, troubled. He was conscious of Charley watching, and he muttered: "Finish checking out that hardware inventory, Charley. I'll be back in a few minutes."

He put on his slicker and hat and followed his son outside.

Jud Brannigan was in his hotel room, shaving. His chin was tilted up to the wall mirror, lather flecking his jaws and throat, when someone knocked on his door.

Brannigan turned and said, still holding the edge of the straight razor to his throat: "Come on in."

Jim Granite stepped inside first, followed by Joe Sequoia. Both men paused, eying their boss with speculative glances.

Granite said with light mockery in his voice:

"Things can't be that bad, Jud."

Brannigan turned back to the mirror; he was in no mood for that kind of humor. Sequoia closed the door. Jim crossed to the window and looked down into the street; a small wind mourned under the eaves.

Joe Sequoia sat down on Brannigan's bed. Jim turned to eye Brannigan. He looked disgruntled.

Brannigan went on shaving. He said coldly: "We were to meet at the Indian Wells relay station. What held you up?"

Granite said shortly: "Bad weather."

Joe Sequoia ran his fingers through raven-black hair. "Thought we had an appointment in Langtry," he said. His eyes ran over the sparsely furnished hotel room. "What are we doing *here?*"

Brannigan rinsed his razor in the bowl of water, then laid it aside.

"Promised a kid a burial," he said.

Joe said: "The Anders boy?"

Brannigan nodded.

Jim Granite turned to him from the window. "That relay station agent didn't have anything good to say about the kid." He eyed Brannigan, frowning. "Is he worth it, Jud?"

Brannigan's voice was cold. "He was a human be-ing, Jim."

Sequoia got to his feet, a faint impatience in his voice. "Well, let's get him buried, then!"

Brannigan dried his face on a towel. "Sure," he said quietly. "Only," his voice turning grim, "there appear to be some objections from the local citizens."

Granite was looking out of the window again. He grinned at Brannigan. "From whom," he said dryly, "we will soon be hearing."

Joe said softly: "Visitor?" and at Granite's slow nod he went to the door and waited, listening.

Brannigan shrugged and picked up a clean shirt. He was slipping it over his head when Sequoia sud-denly jerked the door open.

Frank Mason stood just outside in the hallway, his hand raised to knock. Surprise showed on his heavy face.

"Come in," Joe said. His voice held a light note of maliciousness.

Frank Mason came into the room, and Sequoia closed the door behind him. Granite remained by the window, eying him with cool indifference. Brannigan looked at him but said nothing; he finished tucking his shirt tails into his pants.

He was being deliberately ignored, and this angered Frank Mason. He said harshly: "I'm Frank Mason!"

Brannigan acknowledged the introduction without smiling. "Marshal Brannigan. My partners, Joe Sequoia and Jim Granite."

Frank let his gaze rest briefly on each man. He asked coldly: "The Federal government taking over in Brassada Hill, Marshal?"

Brannigan shrugged. "You know better than that, Mister Mason."

"Then what are you all doing here?"

"We've come to attend a funeral," Sequoia said. His voice was neutral.

Mason swung his attention to him. "Three of you?" There was anger in his eyes. "Three Federal officers here to attend the funeral of a boy none of you really know — a murderer?"

Brannigan cut in coldly: "Was he, Mister Mason?"

The big man turned to him with bleak hostility.

"Everyone in Brassada Hill knows Billy Anders killed Cynthia Choquette —"

Brannigan's voice rode roughly over the freight line owner's. "Everyone *assumes,* Mason! But no one seems to know for sure; no one saw Billy kill her!" He made a hard motion, cutting off Mason's angry reply. "I understand there was no investigation, no attempt to ascertain the truth."

Frank Mason studied Brannigan for a long moment, choking back his anger.

"Tell me, Marshal, you planning to force an investigation on this town?"

Brannigan shrugged. "I'd prefer cooperation, Mister Mason."

"Why?" Mason was puzzled. "What do you want?"

"The truth," Brannigan said.

Mason shook his head. "Billy Anders killed that woman," he said slowly. "Why he killed her doesn't really matter. She was not one of Brassada Hill's most outstanding citizens. But —" he put his gaze on Brannigan, and the anger went out of him all of a sudden. "All right, Marshal, bury him if you want. But leave my family alone!"

"That's what I came here for," Brannigan said. "It's your son who's raising strong objections."

Frank Mason nodded. "I'll talk to him. Roger had reasons for not liking the Anders boy. But Billy's dead now . . . ."

He stopped by the door, putting his hand on the knob. "Bury him wherever you want. I'll pay all the expenses of Billy's funeral."

Brannigan's voice held an icy mockery. "That's generous of you, Mason —"

Mason flared at Brannigan's tone. "Marshal, I happen to own half of this town! What happens in Brassada Hill affects me! I'm trying to avoid needless trouble. Don't goad me, Marshal."

Brannigan said: "Just what are you afraid of, Mister Mason?"

Mason eyed him without answering; something dark and guarded came into his eyes.

Brannigan pressed him. "You don't want us here. Why? Not because of that boy lying on a slab in Sam's back room."

Mason made a bitter gesture of impatience. "I've

been reasonable, Marshal. But if you stay on in Brassada Hill on the pretext of an investigation, then whatever happens will be your sole responsibility!"

He yanked the door open and went out.

Brannigan stood by the washstand, towel in hand. Joe Sequoia closed the door and turned slowly to face Brannigan. By the window, Jim Granite put his questioning, cold gaze on the senior officer.

Brannigan said sharply: "Well, something bothering you boys?"

A faint anger stirred in Joe Sequoia's eyes, but he said nothing. Jim Granite elected to answer.

"Yeah," he said slowly, and brought his hand up to knuckle his jaw. His eyes were hard and direct on Brannigan. There was no disrespect in his tone, but there was opposition.

"We've fought for lost causes before, Jud. Well —" he shrugged —"if you've got something we don't know, some evidence to warrant an investigation, I'm with you. If not —"

Brannigan's temper edged his voice. "If not, what, Jim?"

Granite said stiffly: "If this town hates that kid so

much, why not take him out of here and bury him somewhere else?"

Brannigan said flatly: "No! We're burying him here!"

Granite eased away from the window. He pointed a finger at Brannigan, his voice blunt. "Let's get this straight, Jud. I'm not going to back you just because you're stubborn about this!"

Brannigan turned his gaze on Sequoia. "What about you, Joe?"

Joe shrugged. "Look, Jud," he said quietly, "we've had a long hard ride trying to catch up with you." A smile flickered across his lips. "Almost dinner time and we haven't had breakfast yet."

Brannigan said stiffly: "There's a lunchroom across the street." He turned to Granite. "All right, Jim — you've got a point." But the edge of anger was still in his voice. "I'll tell you why we're staying. Billy Anders was the town's bad boy and its whipping post. When Cynthia Choquette, a madam who ran one of the town's saloons, was killed and Billy ran, no one bothered to question it."

Granite's voice was even. "What was there to question?"

A bleak impatience rode Brannigan's voice. "Why he did it, Jim!" His gaze whipped over to Sequoia. "*If* he did it."

He was silent for a moment, awaiting their reaction. Granite's gaze went to Sequoia. The Cherokee nodded.

Jim said: "Well, let's get going, Jud!"

— IX —
THE LAW TAKES OVER

Sam Hill slowly backed away from his door as the three men pushed their way into the funeral parlor. He had been on his way out and anger stirred in him as Roger Mason wheeled around to face him, his voice curt. "Where is he, Sam?"

The bruises from the recent fight with Billy had all but faded from Roger's face, but his usually good-looking features looked mean this morning. His eyes were bloodshot and his voice was ugly. He had had a bad night; his head ached and his stomach was queasy. But the deep burning hate inside him overrode his discomfort.

Sam said angrily: "I know how you feel, Roger. But

you've no authority —"

Roger took the badge Sheriff Breen had given him from his pocket and pinned it on his coat.

"I have now," he said harshly. "Where is he?"

Sam said: "In there," pointing, and added grimly: "I still don't like it —"

"You don't have to like it!" Roger snarled. "Just do as you're told!"

He nodded to the two men with him. One was a burly warehouse man named Hank who worked for the Masons. The other, a slim townsman named Tom Giles, had been with the posse that had hunted Billy down.

They followed the undertaker into the far back room, and Roger eyed the sheet-covered body with bleak bitterness.

"A box," he said, turning to Sam. "Any kind will do."

Sam gestured to the other room. "All I have are the coffins in there."

Roger glanced inside, his gaze sliding over the coffins ranged along the wall. "The cheapest you have," he said to Sam. "Ill pay you for it."

Sam said: "What are you going to do with him?"

"What do you care?" Roger snapped. "Whatever we do, it'll be better than he deserves!"

Hank and Tom Giles brought the coffin Sam indicated into the embalming room. Roger stood by as they lifted the body off the table and placed him inside the coffin.

Roger said: "Get the wagon backed up to the door, Hank. We'll wait."

The three Federal officers came out of the hotel and paused on the edge of the plank walk, eying the quagmire they had to cross to get to the lunchroom on the other side. Farther down someone had placed planks across the road, providing a sort of narrow catwalk across the street.

They were starting to cross there when Brannigan's attention was drawn to the wagon backed up in front of the funeral parlor.

He said sharply: "Wait!" and wheeled around, the boards squishing under his feet. Jim Granite and Sequoia looked after him.

Two men were coming out of Sam Hill's place, each

man carrying an end of a coffin. The smaller man stepped off into the mud and stumbled. The coffin almost slipped from his grasp, and the burly man cursed.

Tom Giles shifted his hands for a firmer grip and moved forward as Hank heaved his end of the coffin up over the tailgate. He went back to help Giles slide the box all the way inside.

They had it most of the way into the wagon when Hank felt something hard and cold press against his spine. He jerked around and looked into Brannigan's grim face.

"Going somewhere, gentlemen?"

Hank eyed the badge on Brannigan's coat and licked his lips.

Giles turned quickly to shoot a look toward the door as Roger Mason stepped out. Mason reacted to the scene before him; he slipped his hand into his coat pocket and then changed his mind as Jim Granite and Joe Sequoia flanked him. Neither man had drawn his gun; they didn't have to.

Brannigan said thinly: "Billy's body?" and Roger just stared at him, eyes burning.

Brannigan turned to the two men by the coffin. "All right; let's get that coffin back inside!"

Hank and Giles didn't move. Jim Granite took a step toward them. "You heard the man, boys!"

Roger said harshly: "They're under my orders, Marshal! I told you before, stay out of this!"

Brannigan eyed the badge on Roger's coat, and an icy smile rimmed his lips.

"Heading another posse, Mason?"

Roger's voice was stiff. "That badge you're wearing, Marshal, doesn't give you special privileges here. Until Sheriff Breen gets back on his feet, *I'm* the law in Brassada Hill!"

Jim Granite drawled: "Looks like that badge has gone to his head, Jud."

Roger gave him a bitter look.

Hank said uncertainly: "Mr. Mason —"

Brannigan cut him short. "Get that body back inside!"

Hank and Tom Giles glanced at Roger, and the young man nodded sullenly. He stepped aside as they slid the coffin out of the wagon and went back inside with it.

"I don't know why you're doing this, Marshal," Roger said with controlled fury, "but you seem intent on forcing something on this town nobody wants. You don't belong here. I'm sending a wire to the governor right now." His voice rose, flat and bitter now. "We didn't ask for Federal officers here; we don't want you here! Either the governor pulls you out of Brassada Hill, *or we run you out!*"

He jerked his head toward Hank as the burly teamster and Tom Giles came outside.

"Get that team back into the yard, Hank." He turned to Giles. "Thanks for coming along, Tom."

He pushed past Joe Sequoia and went striding angrily up the street toward the telegraph office.

Tom Giles climbed into the wagon with Hank, and they drove off.

Sam Hill stood in the doorway, eying the Federal officers.

He said dryly: "I hope you know what you're getting into, Marshal."

Brannigan turned to him. "Keep your doors locked. Let me know if you have any more trouble —"

Sam shook his head. "Not me, Marshal." He

looked up the street toward the Mason Freight Line. "In fifteen years I've had no trouble here. I intend to keep on living in this town after you're gone."

He took a key ring from a chain anchored to his belt. "Here, the place is yours. You bury Bill Anders. You buck this town—and the Masons."

He tossed the key ring to Brannigan and went off, ducking his head against the drizzle falling like a mist across the street.

Brannigan looked after the undertaker, his face grim.

Joe Sequoia said: "Looks like we're in the undertaking business, Jud."

Brannigan shrugged. "Looks like it." He turned to Granite. "I want somebody in there at all times. You eat first, Jim. Joe goes when you get back."

Jim said: "You joining us?"

"Later," Brannigan said. "I'm going to see a girl first—Billy Anders' girl!"

— X —
"WERE YOU IN LOVE WITH HIM?"

The Mason home was on a broad street in the south end of town. It was a big house, gabled and shuttered in New England style and shaded by old trees. It was set off from the others in the area, with a big barn in back topped by an iron rooster sitting astride a weathervane.

The Masons had been among the first settlers in Brassada Hill, and they had come to town with money.

Brannigan stepped up to the broad covered veranda and used the brass knocker on the oak door. He waited a few moments and tried again. He could hear the sound echo emptily inside, and he frowned, for the moment undecided whether or not to leave and come back later.

The Mason girl could be at the freight line office, but he wanted to see her alone, knowing it would be useless to try to talk to her in the company of her father and brother.

Somewhere in back a big dog began to bark. Brannigan started to turn away; then, on impulse, he tried the door. It wasn't locked. He hesitated, then moved inside.

Virginia Mason was seated in front of the piano in the living room. She had her arms folded across the keyboard, her head resting on her arms. On the piano was another framed picture of her mother in a different pose — this one more formal, stiff and unsmiling.

It was dim in the big room, but the fireplace cast a flickering light, and heat had misted the windows. A small wind muttered under the eaves. Outside, the dog was still barking.

Brannigan eyed the girl. There was an aching loneliness in her that pervaded the room — a sense of despair. He felt like an intruder, and he knew he was. . .

He said after a moment: "Miss Mason?"

She did not stir; she seemed asleep.

He came into the room and raised his voice slightly. "Miss Mason — are you ill?"

She raised her head and turned to him. Her eyes widened, and she stood up abruptly, stepping back from him.

Brannigan had his hat in his hands; he said: "I knocked; guess you didn't hear me. I'm Marshal Brannigan."

She nodded, a dark and nameless fear in her eyes "I know." Her voice was low, colorless. There was no welcome in it.

"You're alone?"

She nodded stiffly. "I'm often alone." Then, her voice cold: "If you're looking for my father or my brother, they're at the freight office."

"I've already talked to them," Brannigan said. He glanced at the picture on the piano.

"Your mother, Miss Mason?"

Virginia looked at him, her voice stiff now, puzzled. "What *do* you want, Marshal?"

Brannigan turned to her. "I want to talk to you — about Billy Anders."

She shook her head. "Why me? I hardly knew him."

Brannigan placed his hat on the piano, took the picture from his coat pocket and held it out to her.

"I'm sure you remember this," he said. "Billy had it with him when he died."

Virginia eyed the creased photo but made no move to take it. She smiled at Brannigan, a small and bitter smile.

"I'm sorry, Marshal. But —"

He cut in quietly: "Were you his girl?"

A startled look flashed into her eyes. She turned away from him, staring into the fireplace. She was silent for a long moment. Outside, the dog had quit barking.

"I — I liked him."

"Were you in love with him?"

Her back was turned to Brannigan, and he could not see the look that came into her eyes, but he saw her frail body stiffen. She clasped her hands in front of her, holding them tightly.

"Love?" Her voice held a strange sadness. "I — we had things in common. Billy was a stray, lonely cat backed against a wall of hate. His fur was up; he was ready to bite at any hand reaching out to him."

She turned now to face Brannigan — a pale girl haunted by memories.

"But he was gentle with me, Marshal — gentle and kind." Her eyes held the lawman, a small flash of defiance stirring in them. "He was not what they say — not as bad as they all say."

"How long did you know him?"

Virginia stood with her back to the fire, finding comfort in the warmth.

"Last winter, at the pond behind Garson's Mill. We had had an unusual freeze. Billy was alone; he was trying to skate on the ice. He kept falling." Her eyes closed for a moment, her thoughts reaching back. "He hated everything, Marshal — even those skates he wore."

She let silence take over, and the defiance faded from her face, leaving her withdrawn and uncaring again.

"He's dead," she said dully. "Why can't you all leave Billy alone?"

"I'm sorry," Brannigan said. "I wish it were that

simple."

She started to turn away from him and he said sharply: "Did Billy kill that woman?"

She stopped, her back to him.

"Did he?"

She turned back to him, a fear in her voice. "Does it matter who killed her? She was a vicious, terrible woman."

Brannigan frowned. "Cynthia Choquette?"

She nodded. "She was cruel and ugly. She didn't belong here. She should never have come to Brassada Hill!"

Brannigan studied her for a moment. "You seem to have known Cynthia Choquette quite well, Miss Mason."

Her gaze flashed to the picture on the piano. Tears made a sudden wet streak on her pale cheeks.

"Leave me alone!" she cried. Then, turning and sobbing: *"Leave me alone!"*

She ran past him, out of the living room and up the stairs to her bedroom. Standing there, Brannigan heard her door slam shut.

He remained awhile longer, looking into the fireplace flames, knowing now there was more to this than a simple burial; knowing that Cynthia Choquette was more than an innocent victim of a shooting.

The answer lay back there in the funeral parlor with Billy Anders and Cynthia Choquette. But Billy was dead, and no one seemed to want to talk about the woman who had run the bawdy house in Brassada Hill. . . .

— XI —
WHO WAS CYNTHIA CHOQUETTE?

Sheriff Breen lay in his bed, staring up at the ceiling. His face was gray, and a film of sweat glistened on his upper lip. He could hear voices beyond his room, but he was not interested. He coughed suddenly, a deep racking sound, and when it subsided he reached for the glass of water on his bedside table.

His wife came in as he settled back on his pillow. "It's that marshal again," she said. "He wants to see you."

He shook his head.

"He wants to talk to you about that woman who was killed."

Breen closed his eyes. "I don't know anything about her," he said. His voice was flat, weary. "Tell him to go away."

She paused in the doorway.

"Floyd —"

He made a motion with his left hand. "Leave me alone!"

She closed the door behind her and went to Brannigan, who was waiting in the front room.

"He's had a bad night," she said. "He doesn't want to see anyone."

Brannigan's smile was cold. "I see. I won't bother him again, Mrs. Breen."

She walked to the door with him.

"It's a thankless job being sheriff," she said. She was a tall woman, her eyes almost on a level with Brannigan's.

Jud nodded. "I imagine it is," he said dryly.

Color spotted her cheeks, but she kept her composure. "I know what you're thinking, Marshal. Floyd took the easy way out about Billy Anders —"

"He deputized a man who hated Billy," Brannigan said evenly. "He didn't have to do that."

"No," she said, "he didn't." Bitterness crept into her voice. "My husband's past the age when he can start again at something else."

"The Masons could do that to him?"

She shrugged. "Maybe. It was a risk he didn't want to take."

Brannigan glanced up the hallway to the bedroom. "So your husband got conveniently sick?" There was an edge of contempt in his voice.

"He is sick, Marshal!" Her voice was cold now. "And there was nothing else he could do, under the circumstances!"

He turned to leave.

"I don't understand, Marshal. A boy who never did anyone any good, and a woman who —"

He turned to look at her. "Did you know Cynthia Choquette?"

Her face stiffened. "Only what the other women in this town knew," she said. "Nothing more."

He was quiet for a moment, thinking. "A madam," he mused. "She is killed, and all of Brassada Hill hates the boy they think killed her." He smiled at the look in her face. "Oh, I know Cynthia Choquette was

discreet in the way she ran her business; I've heard
that from several people. But it was still a bawdy
house she was running, wasn't it, Mrs. Breen?"

"Yes," she said.

"How did you feel about it?"

"Like the other women in this town, Marshal." Her
voice was tight.

"And you did nothing about it?"

She looked away from him now, across the starchy
furniture in the front room. Her voice was distant.
"There was nothing we could do."

He said quietly: "Thank you, Mrs. Breen."

She stood by the door for a long time after Brannigan left, listening to water drip from the eaves. . . .

"Nothing we could do," she whispered, and her
hands clenched, and tears were bitter in her eyes.

A rheumy-eyed swamper opened up as Brannigan
banged on the closed door of the Longhorn Bar.
"We're closed," he said, but Brannigan pushed him
aside and stepped into the barroom. It was gloomy inside; the place was not yet ready for business. Tables
and chairs were stacked in a corner, and a leak in the

roof still dripped water into a pail on the floor.

The swamper was a taciturn, distrustful man. "I don't know anything, Marshal," he said in answer to Brannigan's question. "I just work here."

Brannigan said: "Who owns this place?"

The swamper shrugged and started to turn away with his mop. Brannigan clamped a hand on his shoulder and pulled him around.

"Maybe you'll remember better in jail," he said coldly.

The man's eyes flickered, and a whine came into his voice. "Mister Kenyon owns the place, Marshal. But I don't know —"

"It's all right, Snead. I'll talk to him."

Brannigan turned to face the man who came out of a back room, rubbing sleep from his eyes.

"Been a bad night," Kenyon said pleasantly as he came up. "Didn't sleep well until morning." He glanced at the gray-misted windows. "Won't be much business today, anyway."

He turned to the swamper. "Go ahead — clean up." He walked behind the bar and reached for a bottle on the back shelf. "A little early in the day, Marshal." He held up the bottle. "Join me?"

Brannigan walked up to the bar.

Kenyon poured. "What do you want to know, Marshal? What kind of hell-raiser Billy Anders was?"

"No," Brannigan said softly. "I want to know about Cynthia Choquette."

Kenyon paused with his drink halfway up to his lips. "Why?" He seemed genuinely surprised.

"Did you know her?"

Kenyon shook his head; he took a swallow from his glass and slowly set it down on the bar.

"Not that I didn't go to The Silver Slipper, Marshal. Most of the men in this town did, at one time or another." He shrugged. "But Cynthia kept to herself. I never saw her mingle with the girls or the customers."

"Then why is this town so riled about her death?"

Kenyon frowned. "I guess it's just the combination of everyone hating Billy and her being a woman. And the way she was killed." He grimaced slightly. "Not much left of her face, Marshal."

Brannigan took a swallow of whiskey; it did little to ease the anger in him.

"She ran a business," he said. "Where are all the

help now?"

"Gone," Kenyon said. "Outside of Billy, none of them were from Brassada Hill. The two bartenders and the girls left the day she was killed; took the evening stage."

He started to refill Brannigan's glass, but the lawman put his palm over it.

"Enough for me."

Brannigan thought of the woman lying in the coffin in Sam Hill's mortuary — a strange woman who had come to Brassada Hill six months before and set up shop in a town which was essentially strait-laced.

"She didn't have any special visitors then?" Brannigan asked idly. "Someone from here who knew her before she came to Brassada Hill?"

Kenyon hesitated. "No special visitors, Marshal. But Olin Bates would know —"

"Bates?"

"Tall, thin, reedy sort of man; played piano for her. Odd sort of man. Could play real well, when he wanted to. Wore clothes like a preacher, but of course he wasn't."

"Where is he?"

Kenyon shrugged. "Nobody's seen him since Cynthia was shot. But you might ask Lew Sanders. They seemed to know each other, and it was Lew who got Billy his job in The Silver Slipper."

"I will." Brannigan put a coin on the bar. "Where can I find Sanders?"

"Five miles south of town. Owns a small ranch — he's a bachelor."

He started to slide the coin back to Brannigan. "My treat," he said.

"Thanks, anyway," Brannigan said. "But I make it a habit to pay my way. Avoids trouble later on."

He finished what was left in his glass.

"Must have been a fancy place, The Silver Slipper."

Kenyon nodded. "Lot of imported stuff — chandeliers, bar, drapes."

"The sheriff padlock the place?"

"No," Kenyon said. He put the bottle back on the shelf. "The Masons did — the same night Cynthia Choquette was killed."

Brannigan gave him a long look. "You own this place?"

"Me and the bank," Kenyon said. His voice was uneasy. "Why?"

"Business must have fallen off some when The Silver Slipper opened down the street."

"I made out." A sullen look came into Kenyon's eyes. "If you think I —"

"Killed Cynthia?" Brannigan shrugged. "Hell, everyone knows Billy did it, don't they?"

Kenyon's face lost its pleasantness. "Look, Marshal, I've tried to be helpful —"

"How are you and the Masons getting along?"

Something cold and spiteful flickered in Kenyon's face, but his voice was neutral. "They own the bank. In a way, you can say I work for them. They treat me fine, Marshal."

"Glad to hear it," Brannigan said. He walked to the door and paused. "Lew Sanders' place — south, you say?"

Kenyon nodded. He stood behind the bar, staring at the door, after Brannigan left.

— XII —
LEW SANDERS

The Sanders place was wedged up against a low rocky ridge less than an hour's ride from town. It was not the sort of ranch a man could make money from or even be comfortable on. It was crowded against the hill by the Circle O Ranch, a big outfit whose barbed wire fence Brannigan followed for several miles before it curved northeast away from the Sanders spread.

A man was chopping wood in the yard when Brannigan rode up. He turned and eyed the lawman, the axe held easily in his right hand. He was big, deep of chest, with powerful shoulders. A brown beard hid most of his face, but the eyes that fastened on Brannigan were a startling deep blue.

Just beyond the woodpile a big brindle dog came to his feet, growling low in his throat. He was a savage-looking beast, more wolf than dog. He padded toward Brannigan, and the lawman's horse minced nervously, eying the animal.

Brannigan dropped his hand to his holstered gun. "You, Sanders?"

The big man nodded.

"Call him off!" Brannigan said.

Sanders eyed him for a moment. "King, come back here!"

The dog backed off slowly. Sanders slapped the palm of his hand sharply against his thigh. "Down, King!"

The big brindle sat on his haunches and watched Brannigan dismount. A low growl fluttered in his throat.

"Mean-looking animal," Brannigan said.

Sanders shrugged. "We don't get many visitors." He eyed the badge on Brannigan's coat. "Lawman, eh?"

"Jud Brannigan, United States marshal."

Sanders frowned, and an uneasy look came into his eyes. He glanced toward the house, and Brannigan said: "You alone?"

Sanders nodded. "Just me and King." His voice was sullen. "What do you want?"

"Some information."

Sanders lifted the axe and brought it down on the chopping block, the blade biting deep into the wood.

"I don't know what you're after," he said. "I'm kinda new around here myself. Don't get into town very often —"

"You know a woman named Cynthia Choquette?"

Sanders took a cut of plug tobacco from his pocket and bit into it.

"She's dead," he said. His voice was without feeling.

"But you knew her? Before she came to Brassada Hill?"

Sanders' eyes narrowed. "Someone been telling you things, Marshal?"

Brannigan shrugged. "I've been asking questions."

Sanders let his gaze stray past Brannigan, toward

the town beyond the ridges. "No sense in lying to you then, is there?" He spat out a stream of tobacco juice. "Sure, I knew Cynthia. A long time ago — in New Orleans."

"What was she doing there?"

Sanders grinned. "Ran a bawdy house, same as here."

"Why did she come here?"

Sanders didn't answer. The dog stood up and growled menacingly and looked toward the house, and Sanders said sharply: "Down, King!"

The dog settled back, but he shifted his attention from Brannigan to the house. It was quiet inside the two-room shack, a thin gray curl of smoke issuing from the chimney.

Brannigan frowned. "You got company?"

"No," Sanders said. "The dog's nervous, that's all."

Brannigan was eying the house.

"I don't know why Cynthia came here," Sanders said, and he moved closer to the chopping block, dropping his hand on the axe handle.

Brannigan caught the move, and his eyes went cold. "Does Olin Bates know?"

Sanders' hand tightened on the handle.

"Bates?"

"Probably in there right now, listening," Brannigan said.

Sanders licked his lips. "I don't know anybody named Bates," he said.

"Piano player in The Silver Slipper," Brannigan said. "Disappeared after Cynthia was killed." Brannigan's voice was hard. "Could be he's hiding out here."

"You're crazy!"

"Let's take a look," Brannigan said. He was watching Sanders, and if the big man signaled to the dog, he did not see it.

But the animal came at him in a silent savage run, leaping for his throat. Brannigan drew and fired, the bullets smashing into the animal before it got to him.

He turned in time to see the axe come whirling at him. He ducked and fired a warning shot at Sanders' feet, and the big man stopped, breathing hard, hands clenching helplessly.

Brannigan eyed the dog. "Sorry I had to kill him," he said. He made a motion toward the house. "Let's go inside."

Sanders said harshly: "I told you I was alone!" But he walked in front of the Federal officer toward the house, a big, dangerous man, his long arms swinging by his sides.

It was a small place inside, untidy and still smelling of old cooking. There was a kitchen and a bedroom and a back door leading to a rickety outhouse. Beyond it, jumbled rocks made a maze leading into the ridge.

A man could easily have slipped out that way while they were talking, Branning reflected, and turning to Sanders, he saw a flicker of confirmation in the man's cold blue eyes.

"Satisfied, Marshal?" Sanders' voice was sullen.

"For now." Brannigan nodded.

He didn't like the smell in the house, and he went back outside, keeping the bearded man in front of him.

Sanders stopped by the body of his dog. He was the kind of man who lived alone by preference, a suspicious and surly man living out his days in his own way.

"I raised him from a pup," he said, and there was a bitter anger in his voice as he looked at the lawman.

"You should have kept him on a leash," Brannigan said coldly. He moved to his ground-reined horse. "I didn't come here looking for trouble."

"What are you here for, anyway? Cynthia Choquette is dead. I heard Billy Anders killed her. And a posse caught up with him a couple of nights ago and shot him." Sanders looked puzzled. "What's a Federal officer doing here, asking questions?"

Brannigan shrugged. "I'm not so sure the kid killed her." He saw the look that flashed in Sanders' eyes, and he added casually: "You knew Billy pretty well, didn't you?"

"I knew him."

"Most people in Brassada Hill hated him. Yet you got him a job at The Silver Slipper. Why?"

Sanders' lips curled. "Why not? He was just a wild kid, kicked around by all the good people in town." He looked down at the dog. "He got along fine with King, the few times he visited here."

His gaze met Brannigan's, hard and challenging. "Funny thing about that boy, Marshal; he liked animals."

"But not people?"

Sanders didn't answer this. Brannigan mounted. "What is Olin Bates hiding from?" He shot the question at the bearded man, and for a moment Sanders was unsettled. He stared at Brannigan, his eyes bitter.

"Cynthia Choquette is dead. So is Billy. Let it ride, Marshal. Ain't nothing you can do to bring them back!"

Brannigan said coldly: "I can find out who killed her, Sanders."

He wheeled his mount around and rode off. Sanders watched him until Brannigan dipped out of sight in a ravine angling away from the ridge.

— XIII —
MOVE OVER, INDIAN!

JOE SEQUOIA had finished eating and was having a cigaret with his coffee when the three men came into the lunchroom. They were riders from the big Circle O Ranch, and all three had been with the posse that had hunted Billy Anders down. And like the townsmen, they resented the Federal officers taking over in Brassada Hill.

The big man was named Slade, and he had a cast in one eye, a broken nose and a natural tendency to violence. He came into Meeker's Lunchroom looking for trouble.

He walked directly up to the lawman and tapped

him none too gently on the shoulder, and when Joe Sequoia turned he said contemptuously: "You're on my stool, Indian!"

Joe Sequoia studied him for a moment and then let his gaze move to the two wiry riders flanking Slade. His lips thinned. There were empty stools on either side of him.

But he said pleasantly enough: "Sorry, fella. I didn't know stools were reserved in here."

"You know now," Slade growled.

Sequoia shrugged. He slid onto the stool on his left, dragging his coffee cup with him.

The redheaded rider next to Slade had a nasal twang. "That one, too, Indian!"

Sequoia didn't move. He reached out slowly and butted his cigaret in an ash tray on the counter.

The Mexican counterman backed nervously to the kitchen door and said something in excited Mexican to someone inside. Charley Meeker, the owner of the place, came out and stopped by the end of the counter. Charley did most of the cooking himself and, from the looks of him, enjoyed what he cooked.

He said: "What's going on, Slade?"

Slade gestured to Sequoia. "Didn't know you were letting dogs and Indians into yore place now, Meeker."

Sequoia stood up, facing the big Circle O rider. He said pleasantly: "Then who let you in, mister?"

The big man dropped his hand to his gun, and Joe's Colt made a magic appearance in his hand as he jammed it into Slade's mid-section. It knocked the wind out of the cowboy, doubling him over. Joe jammed his palm into Slade's face and shoved him back across the narrow room.

He was turning to Slade's companions when some-one farther down along the counter threw his coffee cup at Joe. It struck the marshal high up on his left cheek, and the coffee was just hot enough to burn. Joe staggered and lifted a hand to his face, and the red-headed rider lunged for him, knocking the gun out of his hand.

Meeker yelled angrily: "Hold it, Red! I don't want trouble with the law —"

Red backed off, his hand on his gun butt. He glanced at Slade, who was on his feet, still having difficulty breathing.

Joe said grimly: "Assaulting a United States marshal is a Federal offense," and started to pick up his gun. Red's companion kicked it away from him, and Slade, pushing past Red, snarled: "I'll handle this, Red!"

He went charging into Joe, slamming the slighter lawman against the counter, loosening it from its moorings. Cups and dishes rattled dangerously. Slade's big hand clawed at Sequoia's face. The wiry lawman wrestled himself free and brought his knee up into Slade's crotch. The burly rider doubled sharply, his face draining of blood. Sequoia brought his locked hands down hard across Slade's neck.

The big Circle O rider slumped to the floor.

Red drew and was ready to shoot when Meeker's shotgun blast into the floor spun him around.

"I said that's enough!" the lunchroom owner yelled. "I ain't having a killing in my place!"

Red eyed the twin barrels pointed at him and decided not to challenge Meeker. He shrugged and slipped his Colt back into the holster.

Meeker pointed to Slade on the floor. "Pick him up and take him out of here! And if you know what's good for you, you'll go back to your ranch and stay there!"

Joe waited, his back by the counter. There was a sharp pain in his side, and his lower lip was cut where Slade had butted him. He fingered a bruise under his eye where the coffee cup had hit him and watched as the two sullen Circle O men hauled Slade to his feet and took him outside.

He turned to the restaurant owner. He started to say, "Thanks —"

But Meeker cut in curtly: "If you're through, Marshal —"

Joe's smile froze on his lips. "I'm through." He put money on the counter, picked up his Colt and walked out.

Jim Granite was sitting at Sam's desk, thumbing through a mortician's trade journal, when Joe came in. He tossed the magazine aside and stood and stretched, his fingertips reaching nearly to the ceiling.

"Was beginning to think you'd gotten lost," he said. His tone was casual.

Joe walked past him and looked into the inner room. "Jud back yet?"

Granite shook his head as Joe turned to look at him. "Been gone a long time," Joe commented. He sucked on a loose tooth for a moment. "Anyone bother you?"

Jim said: "Quiet as the inside of a church." He eyed the bruise under Joe's eye. "Tough dinner?"

Joe smiled coldly. "They don't like Indians in this town, Jim."

Something hard and flinty came into the ex-mountain man's eyes. He said softly: "Don't they now?" and joined Joe in the doorway and glanced into the room where Cynthia Choquette lay in her coffin.

The silence ran between them for a long moment; there were no windows in that room, and even with the sun out it was gloomy. Someone, Sam maybe, had placed candles at the head of the casket. The flames flickered under some vagrant breeze.

Joe said: "How's the wake?"

Jim shrugged. "I barred the back door," he said, "just in case."

Joe walked to Sam's desk and picked up the magazine Jim had discarded. "This all there is to read around here?"

The older man gave him a quizzical look. "Didn't know Indians were that particular." He walked to the door. "How was the chow?"

"Kinda stuck in my throat," Joe replied. His face was impassive. "Maybe you'll have better luck."

Jim nodded. "We'll see."

Joe Sequoia picked up his rifle and stood by the window as Jim went out. There was a mist on the windowpanes; he wiped a clear spot and looked out.

Riders were coming into town in twos and threes; small clusters of people stood on the plank walks, watching.

Brannigan had been gone a long time, he thought; something could have happened to him. The big marshal was capable enough, but this town was like a powder keg, waiting only for a spark to set it off.

He turned and glanced back toward the curtained doorway. A kid back there, dead and waiting to be buried, was the cause of it all.

Joe Sequoia shook his head in disbelief.

— XIV —
"NEXT MAN GETS SHOT!"

Jim Granite walked with the long easy stride of a mountain man. He headed down the street, away from the lunchroom, wanting to work the stiffness from his sinewy body, liking the feel of the fine mist in his face.

He had lived a half-dozen lives before becoming a Federal officer. He had lived with the Utes and the Oglallas for a while and had taken a squaw for a wife; she had died in childbirth. He had been miner and guide and surveyor, and twice he had gone up the trail to Dodge City as a trail hand, liking the wildness and the camaraderie of the cattle drives.

Jim had a lone wolf's way of looking at things. He

didn't know Billy Anders, but he knew what it was to be unwanted.

He still liked the far places, the lost and lonely places. He didn't like towns or the people in them, and anything more than two or three buildings crowded him. Death he accepted in the natural course of things; he had his own code of justice. If he had his way he'd go by the old Judaic law of "an eye for an eye." But Brannigan lived by today's law, and he was a tough enforcer of it.

Jim was a little irked by Brannigan's seeming secretiveness. But Jud was the boss, and he had his prerogatives. . . .

The tall man wheeled across the street now, feeling the looseness come back into his step. He was a man of great zest, and now his appetite began to take on an edge. He was striding past the closed door of The Silver Slipper when he thought he heard someone playing a piano inside. He tried the door, and the tinkling stopped. *Or was it his imagination?*

The wind freshened as he walked, and the fine mist gathered in drops on his face and ran down the bridge of his nose. His thoughts ran on ahead of the town —

to Langtry, close to the Mexican Border. They were expected there, and he suspected there would be trouble from the regional office when they didn't show up.

But Brannigan had a free-wheeling way about him. That was how he handled his job, and that was what Joe and Jim Granite liked about him. . . .

Jim came back up the plank walk toward Meeker's Lunchroom. People avoided him, stepping into doorways as he came up; women turned their heads. Jim grinned sourly.

There was a cluster of men gathered around the open-fronted blacksmith shop. They were eying Sam Hill's Funeral Parlor across the street.

Jim slowed his stride. "All right, folks." His voice was a slow drawl. "Break it up!"

Mike, the blacksmith, stood angrily by his forge, bellows in hand. The coals were getting cold. He had a couple of horses to shoe, but they could wait. He was a big hairy man except for his head, which was billiard-ball bald under his hat.

He said harshly: "Marshal, you got no right —"

Jim's hand drifted to his gun. "Get moving!"

The men started to move away, sullen and dragging their feet.

Mike glared at Jim, but the lawman's gaze held steady, his hand still on his gun. Angrily, the blacksmith began pumping air into the coals. . . .

Jim walked on toward the lunch room. There was a quiet anger in the town that he did not like. He was about to go inside when he saw Jud Brannigan turn the corner and come riding toward him.

He waited, and Jud swung into the rack in front of him and dismounted. Brannigan, Jim thought, looked tired.

Brannigan said shortly: "Joe eat?" and Jim nodded.

"Join me, Jud?"

"Not hungry," Brannigan replied. "But coffee'll do fine."

They went inside.

A lone customer was sucking soup from a bowl at the far end of the counter. Meeker was seated at a small table, going over his books. He chewed on a stub of cigar, his underwear showing through his unbuttoned shirt. His counterman was in the kitchen, peeling potatoes.

Meeker looked up as the lawmen entered. He wasn't friendly. Brannigan and Granite eyed the buckshot scars in the floor, and Brannigan turned quickly and shot a questioning look at Jim, who shrugged.

"Joe had some trouble," he said.

"Bad?" Brannigan's eyes glinted dangerously.

"A fat lip and a mouse under his eye," Jim replied sourly.

Brannigan relaxed. They walked to stools and sat down and waited as Meeker took his time before coming up to wait on them.

The lunchroom owner said: "Bad time to eat. Haven't much choice." He glanced toward the door "I suggest you try the hotel dining room, or maybe the Chink's place on Badwater Street."

Brannigan cut him off: "You've got coffee?"

Meeker nodded sullenly and looked at Jim.

Granite said: "I'm a growing boy. See if you can't rustle up some meat — steak if you have it, roast beef, hash — and all the potatoes you have left. A half-dozen biscuits should do it."

Meeker eyed him for a moment, then went into the

kitchen.

Brannigan sipped his coffee.

Jim said: "Find out anything?"

Brannigan frowned. "Enough to convince me the kid didn't kill the woman." He was silent for a moment. "The Masons are tangled up in it. They closed The Silver Slipper, sort of took over when the Choquette woman was killed. Maybe they owned it, too — they seem to own 'most everything else in Brassada Hill."

Jim whistled softly.

"The Masons — owning that kind of place?"

Brannigan nodded. "A place nobody liked publicly, but it was privately patronized by most of the men in town." He finished his coffee. "I might know more if I could find a man named Olin Bates. He used to play the piano in The Silver Slipper."

Granite frowned. "Piano player? I thought I heard someone playing when I walked by The Silver Slipper."

"You sure?"

Granite considered. "No, not sure."

Meeker brought him his steak and potatoes and biscuits. Brannigan walked to the end of the counter, where a cigar box stood open by an old cash register. He picked out a cigar and, lighting it, went back to join Jim.

Meeker watched them silently from the table in back.

Granite finished his late dinner, and drained his coffee cup. Brannigan paid for both.

They went outside, Granite chewing on a toothpick. Both men paused to eye the crowd, which had gathered again in front of the blacksmith shop.

Granite commented dryly: "Never thought a dead man could stir up so much trouble."

Brannigan shrugged, his voice cold, cynical. "The Lord forgives us our sins, but not our fellow man."

They started to walk toward the funeral parlor, going past the silent, hostile men. As they went by, someone said angrily: "Look at them! Like they own the town!"

Jim jerked his head around, but could not spot the man. Brannigan ignored the whole thing and kept on walking. They crossed the street and were coming up to the funeral parlor when a thrown horseshoe came wheeling in just ahead of them, smashing through the mortuary glass.

Jim Granite wheeled like a mountain cat. The burly blacksmith stood on the walk, his muscled forearms bared. He made no effort to conceal the fact he had thrown the shoe.

Jim Granite broke into a run toward the blacksmith shop.

Brannigan said sharply: "Jim, wait!"

But Granite wasn't listening. The burly blacksmith stood his ground. He was a powerfully built man and a mean fighter. He squared off as the lawman came running up. Jim grabbed a fistful of his shirt and said through his teeth: "Mister, don't you ever try anything like that again!"

Mike shoved the lawman off and made a grab for the nearest object at hand, which happened to be the tongs in the forge. He took a savage, two-handed swipe at Granite's head with it.

The crowd scattered out of the way as the lawman ducked. Jim brought his knee up into the blacksmith's crotch, and when the man doubled he clamped a hold on Mike's left arm and brought it up sharply behind his back. Mike's face squeezed with pain as a bone snapped.

Standing a few feet away, Hank, the Mason warehouse man, grabbed a horseshoe from a rack and slammed it at Granite. The shoe caught the marshal between his shoulder blades and sent him staggering, falling over Mike.

Granite rolled over, the breath knocked out of him. His hand fumbled for his Colt as other angry men surged toward him.

Hank picked up a hammer. "Come on," he said wildly. "Let's run them out of town now!"

He took a step toward Granite and then collapsed as a gun barrel slammed across his head. Brannigan whirled, eyes bleak, gun ready....

From across the street, standing in the doorway of the mortuary, Joe Sequoia fired a warning rifle shot over that angry mob's head!

The crowd surged back.

Brannigan warned harshly: "Next man who makes a move gets shot!"

He backed toward Jim, who was slowly getting to his feet. Brannigan said: "You all right, Jim?"

His partner nodded; he was having difficulty

breathing.

Mike was crawling toward his back door, his left arm limp. He turned and pulled himself up to his feet and stared at the lawmen, his face a mask of pain and hate.

Brannigan bent over Hank, who was stirring. He yanked the barely conscious man to his feet and shoved him into the arms of the nearest onlooker.

"Get him home!" It was a flat order. "And the rest of you move out of here, or I'll jail the lot of you for unlawful assembly and riot!"

The crowd stood sullen, hostile; a few men started to drift away.

Brannigan thumbed back the hammer of his drawn Colt. "I said to break it up!"

Then he turned his head as a man farther up the street said sharply: "Hold it, Marshal. You're not giving any more orders here!"

Roger Mason was coming at a run, waving a telegram. He stopped in front of Brannigan, his face flushed, breathing heavily.

"This is for you!" He held the telegram under

Brannigan's nose. "You no longer have any authority here!" He turned to the watching men. "You don't have to leave! You don't have to do anything he says!"

He turned back to Brannigan. "Go on," he snarled. Read it!"

Brannigan took the telegram, flicked his cold gaze over it and handed it back.

"Wire the governor my regrets," he said grimly. "We're staying!"

Roger Mason stiffened, his gaze showing disbelief. "You're disobeying a state order?"

Brannigan nodded. "I'm making this a Federal case."

"You mean you're not going?"

Brannigan nodded. "We're burying Anders in Brassada Hill!"

A wild and bitter expression flared up in Mason's eyes. "You're crazy, Brannigan!" He whirled and swept his arm in a gesture that took in most of the town. "Take a good look, Marshal! Nobody in this town wants you here! You've got no authority — even the governor wants you out! You still feel big enough to buck us — all of Brassada Hill?"

"All of Texas, if I have to!"

Brannigan's cold, stubborn smile unsettled Mason. "It doesn't make sense. All this, for a killer who never was any good?"

"Billy Anders didn't kill Cynthia Choquette!" Brannigan said flatly. "That's why we're staying!"

Mason's distorted features came together in a bitter mask.

"All right, Marshal," he said thickly. "I've tried to reason with you, bent over backwards to get you out of here. Now we'll have to do it another way."

He pointed a savage, rigid forefinger at Brannigan. "We're giving you and your men until midnight to take Billy and ride out of here! If you're still here, we're coming in after him. And if you try to stop us, we'll bury all of you with him — out in a hole in the hills, where you all belong!"

— XV —
THE DECISION

THE FINE MIST persisted as the day ended. Brassada Hill was like a town that had died. It was very still, very quiet. One could hear water drip from eaves all over town.

Frank Mason came into the freight office and walked to the window. He stared out into the muddy street, his thoughts turned inward, his shoulders sagging, like a man carrying a great weight.

Charley Springer was making entries in his ledger, going over invoices.

Frank said: "Go on home, Charley!"

The clerk turned on his stool, surprised.

"I'm closing early tonight."

Charley closed the book and placed his quill pen back in its holder. He went to the rack and took his coat and hat off a hook and put them on.

"Shall I open up same time in the morning?"

"If there is a morning." Frank's voice sounded very tired.

Charley eyed the big man for a moment, then went out, closing the door silently behind him.

Frank remained at the window, a big man caught up in his past, rendered powerless by events he could not have foreseen. . . .

His son was out there somewhere, a boy he no longer could control — a man he could not reason with. In the space of one short week, Roger Mason had changed from an easygoing, obedient boy to a man he no longer understood.

Frank knew what he should do, what he should have done right away, when Brannigan brought Billy's body back to town. It had been in his power to stop what was now happening. But he realized it was too late now.

He couldn't face his son with the truth, nor could he

face Brassada Hill. He had built up too much of a stake here, and it had entrapped him.

He listened to the muttering of the lonely wind as the clouds overhead began to break up. The storm had blown over in the sky above the town, but a new storm was gathering in Brassada Hill, and only morning would assess the damages. . . .

Joe Sequoia stood by the mortuary window, rifle held firmly in his hands, and peered through the boards barring the shattered glass. No one moved out in the street. There were faint sounds of men talking from somewhere beyond his range of vision. As he watched, a wagon rolled out of town, a farmer and his wife sitting stiffly on the seat.

Someone was hammering in back, and Joe turned and walked to the embalming room, pausing in the doorway to watch Jim Granite hammer the last plank in place across the back door. The window was already boarded up.

The still figure under the sheet was vague in the gathering dusk. There was a lamp on a small table beyond, and Joe lighted it, turning the wick down.

Granite swung around to face him, hammer in hand. "Boarded up tight," he growled. "If they're going to come at us, they'll have to come from the street side."

He tossed the hammer aside and joined his partner, and they walked back to the office.

Joe glanced up at the wall clock above Sam's desk. "He's been gone a long time, Jim."

Granite frowned. "I didn't hear any shooting —"

"A knife doesn't make any noise," Joe said. There was no humor in his voice. He glanced at the door. "We'll give him five more minutes. Then I'll go see what's keeping Jud —"

"You'll stay right here," Jim growled. And at Joe's look, he added: "Hell, you know how this town feels about Indians. No sense in sticking your neck out —"

Joe moved up to the window and was silent, looking out.

Granite knuckled the bristle on his jaw. "Hope Jud is right, Joe."

"About the kid back there?"

Jim nodded.

Joe glanced toward the back door. "Open and shut

case. That's what this town believes. Brannigan seems to be the only man who doesn't —"

The clock on the wall struck eight with slow, measured strokes.

Jim picked up his rifle. "Hold the fort, Joe." He started for the door, but brought up short as footsteps sounded outside. A fist rapped on the door.

Brannigan's voice said: "Open up!"

Jim slipped the bolt back, and Brannigan came inside. His face was grim.

"They've gotten to the telegraph office," he said. "It was closed. The operator's gone home. I broke inside, but the wire's out. I couldn't reach the governor."

There was a heavy silence for a moment; then Granite bolted the door and turned to Brannigan.

"Where does that leave us, Jud?"

"Out on a limb, I reckon." Brannigan's voice was wry.

Joe said: "Not if we play it their way and pull out with the kid's body."

Brannigan put a hard, cold look on the lawman. "That your vote, Joe?"

Joe's face was impassive; he shook his head.

Granite met Brannigan's questioning gaze. "I've already signed up for the wake," he said mildly.

Brannigan started to pace, his eyes hard. "They've got the governor on their side. If we stay on, what happens tonight will legally be our fault, unless —"

He paused, frowning.

"Unless what, Jud?"

Brannigan put his gaze on Granite. "Unless I can prove Billy Anders didn't kill the Choquette woman."

Joe glanced at the clock. "You've got less than four hours."

Brannigan faced the fact. He sighed, shook his head. "Maybe I'm wrong, boys. Maybe I'm being too stubborn. The kid's dead."

Jim cut in quietly: "You still looking for a piano player?"

Brannigan eyed him.

Granite smiled and made a motion with his hand. "Come along."

Brannigan and Joe followed him to the back room. The lamp cast flickering shadows across Billy's covered body.

Granite paused by the boarded back door. "Listen, Jud."

It was quiet in the room, it was quiet in Brassada Hill, and because of this the sound carried. Somewhere beyond that back door, in the direction of The Silver Slipper, someone was softly playing a piano; someone who knew how to play, who loved to play.

Brannigan whirled.

"We're staying!" he decided grimly. "Hold them off! I'll be back before midnight!"

Joe said quietly: "What if you're not?"

Brannigan looked from him to Granite. "*I* promised that boy a funeral in Brassada Hill — not you! If I'm not back before they come for him — make your own decision!"

Joe said: "We'll wait, Jud."

Granite nodded.

— XVI —
OLIN BATES

The Silver Slipper lay dark and quiet in the night. Candlelight flickered, casting a small and uncertain glow over the empty room. The shadows seemed to hold within their shifting embrace the remembrance of things past, the faint echoes of laughter long forgotten.

Olin Bates sat on the piano stool in a corner by the curving staircase — a sad-faced man in shirt sleeves, a bowler hat cocked back on his head. He wore a striped silk shirt, and gaudy armbands tight around his biceps held the sleeves back from his wrists.

He was a man past youth and past conquests, a

man looking back in time to better days. He was playing with his eyes half closed, remembered pain and ecstasy etched into his dissolute face.

Someone rapped on the window. He came out of his rapt state, and his hand went to his gun on the piano, by his half empty whiskey glass. He turned and stared toward the window, but could see nothing. After a moment he got up and shuffled toward the door, gun in hand.

He slanted his gaze through the rain-misted window and saw a man's figure bulking dark and indistinct. Then, as the man outside moved, something on his coat glinted. The sad-faced man smiled expectantly and unbolted the door, opening it to eye the man in front of it.

"What can I do for you, Marshal?"

"Olin Bates?"

The piano player nodded.

Brannigan's voice was blunt. "Let me in."

Bates unhooked the heavy chain and swung the door wide. Brannigan pushed past him and walked into the big room.

Even in the flickering candlelight, it was a gaudy

room, with back-bar mirrors and crystal chandeliers and a long and highly polished cherrywood bar. But already the dust of neglect was beginning to settle, softening the patina of polished wood, hazing the mirrors. Chairs and tables were stacked in corners, and a sad air of disuse hung like a shroud over the room.

Olin Bates said softly: "I was expecting you, Marshal."

Brannigan dropped his gaze to the gun in Bates' hand, and the sad-faced man shrugged. He walked to the piano and placed the gun down, saying quietly: "This wasn't for you."

"Someone else?"

Bates' smile had a wicked flash to it. "Brassada Hill isn't exactly a peaceful place right now, as you should know, Brannigan."

"They said the place was closed," Brannigan said.

Bates nodded. "Closed, and already forgotten. Everyone gone — the bartenders, the girls — even the swamper."

"But you've stayed?"

Bates smiled. "I've elected myself caretaker. Someone has to watch over this place until it's disposed of."

"The Masons own it?"

Bates looked surprised. "Not that I know of." He took a sip from his glass. "In fact, I'd swear they didn't."

"They closed the place down, right after Mrs. Choquette died —"

"Miss Choquette," Bates corrected gravely. Then, his lips twisting wryly: "The Masons do pretty much as they like in Brassada Hill."

"So I've heard," Brannigan murmured. He looked about the dark and empty room, trying to picture it as it had been before it was closed.

Bates ran his fingers lightly across the piano keys. "You can't see it now, the way it is, Marshal. But there wasn't a place in New Orleans that was better. A little fancier, maybe, but not better."

"A bawdy house," Brannigan muttered. "Fancy or plain, they're just the same."

Bates shrugged. "I was in Lew Sanders' place when you rode out this morning."

Brannigan looked at him. "I figured you were."

"Too bad about the dog. He was the only thing Sanders cared for."

Bates picked up his glass and drained what was left.

"You ran out and hid after Miss Choquette was killed," Brannigan said. "Why did you come back?"

Bates was silent for a moment, thinking. "I guess I knew you'd find me. Maybe I even wanted you to find me — before someone else does."

He picked up the candle and his glass from the piano and walked across the room with them, the shadows shifting as he walked. Brannigan watched him stop in front of the bar. He placed the candle on the counter, and the small light reached up to illumine a large oil painting hanging behind the bar.

He turned and said: "Drink, Marshal?" When Brannigan shook his head, he went around the bar, took a bottle from the back shelf and poured himself a stiff drink.

Brannigan walked slowly to the bar and, placing his foot on the brass rail, watched the sad-faced man put the bottle back. It was quiet and dark in The Silver Slipper, and the silence between them was heavy with things unsaid. He knew Bates was getting ready to tell him what he knew, but Brannigan knew that he could not push the man.

So he looked up, studying the oil painting in an ornate gilt frame.

"Cynthia Choquette?"

Bates nodded.

"A beautiful woman," Brannigan said, and his comment was sincere.

Olin glanced up at the painting. "Yeah." He took a long swallow from his glass. Brannigan had the feeling he had been drinking steadily for some time now, but it didn't show.

"Cynthia Choquette, twenty years ago. So she said —"

"Changed?"

Bates looked at him. "And then some."

Brannigan frowned. "How long did you know her?"

"About three years — in New Orleans. Played piano for her there. Came with her when she sold out and moved here six months ago."

He looked up at the portrait again, the sadness

deepening in his voice. "The years must have been hard on her, Marshal. She didn't look much like that even when I first knew her."

He refilled his glass.

"She used to come out here after the customers had gone. She'd stand right where you're standing now and look up at that painting, hating herself—or maybe hating somebody else. I couldn't tell."

"And Billy Anders killed her?"

Olin shrugged. "Must have."

"But you didn't see him do it?"

"No one saw it," Bates said. He walked back to the piano with his glass and stood by it, brooding. "I was out when it happened . . . ."

He turned and looked at Brannigan across the still room. "I knew the kid. He used to come to work like some stray mongrel, glad for a few scraps of affection, but bristly if anyone approached him. Guess that's why Sanders liked him. Even got him a job here. And maybe that's why Cynthia hired him. She was a strange woman. She hated this town, the people in it."

"Yet she left New Orleans to come here?"

Bates was silent for a moment.

"She must have had a reason for coming."

"Lew knew her from way back," Bates said. "He sent her a letter in New Orleans. I don't know what was in it; she burned it right after she read it. But that was when she decided to come to Brassada Hill."

"What did she do here?"

"Far as I know, nothing she didn't do back in New Orleans." Bates waved carelessly toward a door barely visible beyond the bar.

"Her room. Combination office, parlor and bedroom. Private entrance on the alley." He paused, his lips twisting in a faint smile. "Cynthia wasn't young any more. But she had her own callers."

"Roger Mason ever come in here?"

Olin shook his head. "Not him, Marshal. His kind's too good, if you know what I mean." He smirked. "But his sister now — she was different."

Brannigan remembered the pale slip of a girl he

had talked to in the Mason house . . . .

"She came here?"

"Oh, not in *here!*" Olin said quickly. "But she used to meet the Anders boy out back. Once I thought I heard her in Cynthia's room; sounded like they were having an argument. But you never knew about Cynthia. She had violent moods, and sometimes she yelled for nothing."

Brannigan let his glance run across the dim and empty room to Cynthia Choquette's closed door.

"Was the Mason girl in here when Cynthia was killed?"

Olin took a swallow from his whiskey glass. He made a wry face. "Funny thing you should ask, Marshal —"

"Was she?" Brannigan's voice was grim.

"Yes. Cynthia sent me to fetch her brother, Roger. I don't know why she wanted him. I never saw him in here, and I didn't even know she knew him. It was after Billy and Roger had a fight; maybe it had something to do with that. But when Cynthia was in one of her moods, I didn't question her."

"Did Roger come here?"

Bates shook his head. "Virginia Mason came instead!"

— XVII —
THE VIGIL

Peering through a slit on the boarded window, Joe Sequoia could see the moon shine through a break in the clouds. It was a Cheyenne moon, and it hung like a Saracen blade over Brassada Hill.

Joe watched it for a long moment, old memories stirring in his dark and impassive face. Then he pulled back and turned to Jim, who was seated in a chair slanted back against the wall, his rifle across his knees. Jim's hat was tipped over his eyes; his head was resting on his chest. But Joe knew the man was not sleeping.

Jim Granite had the habit of resting like a mountain cat, eyes closed, but ears cocked, some inner alertness attuned to whatever went on around him.

Restless, Joe walked to the curtained doorway and looked in at Cynthia's casket. The candles placed at the head of the coffin were burning low; the tiny flames flickered under some vagrant breeze, and one of them went out.

There were spare candles in the room, but Joe was not inclined to replace it. He stood looking beyond the cloth-draped bier to where Billy Anders lay, and he was surprised to find himself in sympathy with the wild youngster who had wanted only to be buried in the town where he had grown up.

"Life sure has its odd moments, Joe."

Joe turned and saw Granite looking at him from under his hat brim.

Joe shrugged.

"Two of us standing wake over someone we didn't even know."

Granite sighed, pulled his hat back over his eyes and slowly let his head fall back on his chest.

Joe drifted back to the shattered window. He stood for a moment, listening to the night wind outside.

"I wonder what the kid did to make Roger Mason hate him so much."

He got no answer from Jim; he had not really expected any. He moved restlessly around the room, belying old wives' tales of Indians' patience. He was not a stolid man. And he envied Jim's ability to settle back and wait.

He picked up the magazine from the desk and then tossed it back. Even at a better time it was not the kind of thing he'd read.

He started to look through the desk drawer and then froze. He thought he heard a noise from the back room, and he shot a look at Jim. But the long-framed man was quiet and didn't move.

Restless and wary, he went into the back room and stood by the door. The town was like a morgue, he thought, and the description brought wryness to his face.

He listened, but could no longer hear the piano from The Silver Slipper — *if* it had come from The Silver Slipper.

He wondered if Brannigan had gotten inside, and if he had, what he was doing. He knew the big lawman well enough to trust his judgment. But Jud had not been too clear about things. However, Brannigan had promised Billy a burial there, and Joe knew Brannigan was a stubborn man when it came to keeping promises.

He went quiet-footed back to the office and looked out into the street as several riders came by the mortuary, turning to stare with cold and hostile eyes at the boarded window. They rode on, passing out of Joe's angle of vision.

The whole atmosphere in town was now one of gathering violence. Joe turned and eyed the clock over Jim's head just as it started to strike ten.

Damn it, he thought. *What was Brannigan doing?*

Cynthia Choquette's room was gaudy and pretentious and overly frilly, as though its recent occupant had been both child and vixen and vain beyond measure. A big four-poster bed took up part of the big room, its canopy bordered in frilly purple velvet.

An ornate dresser and mirror faced the foot of the bed, its padded velvet stool still dusted with face powder from a mishap or a burst of petulant anger.

There were perfumes and bottles of lotions and jars of creams aplenty; almost every conceivable concoction, most of them foreign, to keep a woman young and beautiful forever. The inscriptions on the bottles said so. But they lied.

Cynthia Choquette might have been beautiful once, but according to Olin Bates, when she died she had been grossly fat, pouch-eyed, wrinkled — and unmourned.

Brannigan was kneeling before a horsehide-covered trunk next to a French Provincial chaise longue. The lid was flipped back. There was an assortment of items: old fans, lacy and frilly and expensive; shawls, sea shells from some forgotten and distant Pacific shore, cheap memorabilia — all things belonging to Cynthia's past, to moments in time, forever lost....

As the lawman started to dig deeper into the trunk, Olin said uneasily: "I don't mind you going through her things, Marshal. But I hope you have the authority."

Brannigan didn't bother to answer him. His groping fingers found and came up with a rolled sheet of paper. It was yellowed with time and tied in the middle with a strip of blue ribbon.

Olin looked down over Brannigan's shoulder. "She kept a lot of things in there she never used. I never saw her open it; she never bothered to lock it. What she had of valuables she kept locked up in the safe." He pointed to the squat iron box in a corner of the big room. It stood beside her desk and was disguised by a yellow scarf covering the top and hanging down the sides. It held a vase with flowers, but they were withered now, the petals fallen.

Brannigan nodded absently as he untied the ribbon and rolled the paper out in his hand. It had not been looked at in a long time, he thought; time and heat had dried it out, and it cracked between his fingers.

He studied it for a long time, his face impassive. Olin Bates said: "Can't be anything important, Marshal — not in there."

Brannigan rolled the sheet of paper up again and retied it with the faded blue ribbon. He slipped it into his coat pocket.

"No," he said tonelessly. "Not very important."

Olin followed him out to the shadowy barroom. The small stage in back was quiet, the curtains hanging limply, the candlelit footlights dark. By the piano, the staircase swept up to the cribs on the second floor. Along its polished banister scantily clad girls had lounged, waiting for customers. The heavy silence seemed to hold faint echoes of what had been....

Brannigan stopped by the bar and looked up at the portrait of Cynthia Choquette.

He said: "I'll have that drink now, Olin."

— XVIII —
DARKENING SHADOWS

The Longhorn Bar was crowded. Most of the men in Brassada Hill were there, and some of the riders from outlying ranches. They drifted in and out of the place, some of them uneasy and not wanting to be part of the trouble brewing in town, but all of them sympathizing with Roger Mason. By the time it turned dark, a hard-core group of more than a score of men remained, listening to Roger, who stood with his back to the bar, his face distorted with the intensity of his emotions.

"You all know what's happened! Three men have taken over *our* town! Three men are trying to ram their authority down our throats!"

He pointed to Hank, who was wearing a bandage under his hat. "Pistol-whipping those who dare to speak out against them, defy them—"

The men murmured angrily. But there was still a reluctance in the crowd, a holding back—and Roger sensed it.

"You know and I know what Billy Anders was!" Roger went on. He spoke of Billy as though he were referring to some animal. "Are we going to let these men have their way? Let them bury Billy here, among our own?"

The crowd stirred, reacting with uneasy resentment. But a tall, thin man ventured a halting dissent.

"Could be some of us will get killed, Mr. Mason, just to keep them from burying the boy —"

Roger whirled on him, his face ugly in that moment of wild passion.

"My mother's buried there, Al — *my mother!*"

Al fell silent before the unreasoning glare in Roger's eyes. Slowly the younger man regained some measure of control; he turned to run his glance over the others.

"All of you have kinfolk in the cemetery. Do *you* want a killer like Billy Anders among them, fouling up the ground they lie in?"

His words whipped at the reluctant crowd. The rumbles of anger grew louder.

Roger railed at them. "Well, that's what Brannigan and his men are going to do, if we let them have their way —"

Sam Hill pushed through the crowd to face Roger. He had come in late, and the mood of the mob disturbed him.

"Wait a minute," he said. "I'm not for them, either, Roger. They've taken over my place; they're holed up in there right now. But they're United States marshals. We can't treat them like outlaws —"

"Can't we?" Roger snarled. He held up the telegram he had received. "It's right here! The governor ordered them to leave. Brannigan refused. It's up to us now to drive them out!"

Al Reisling said: "That won't be easy, Mr. Mason. They've got guns. And like Sam said, they're forted up in his place —"

"There are all the rifles we need in the sheriff's office," Roger cut him off. "I've got the keys. And there's a keg of gunpowder in my father's storeroom —"

"For God's sakes!" Sam yelled. "Governor or no governor, they're still Federal officers!" He swung around to Roger. "You'll be leading a lynch mob if you —"

Roger brushed him aside. "Listen, all of you! Sheriff Breen is still confined to his bed. I'm the law in Brassada Hill, duly appointed. And we've got the guns!" His intensity carried to the liquor-frenzied crowd. "Come on, boys — let's use them!"

Sam tried to stop them as they surged after Roger, but he was swept aside . . . .

Frank Mason walked slowly along the deserted street to his house. The wind had freshened after the wild storm that had battered Brassada Hill, and although it was not cold, it sent a chill through him. He paused to look back toward the center of town. In the stillness, he could hear the mutter of angry, indistinguishable voices, and he knew they were coming from the Longhorn Bar.

He felt ill. He had waited in the office for Roger to return. He had waited in the dark, staring bleakly into the night, going over his past, like a man awaiting a firing squad at dawn.

He knew then that Roger was beyond recall. He had gone to the Longhorn to see him and had been turned away. He walked with dragging steps now, pushing open the wrought-iron gate and moving up the flagstone walk, past flower beds that had long since been neglected. Virginia had taken care of them for a while, after his wife died . . . .

He opened the door and placed his coat and hat on the hall rack and went into the parlor. It seemed cold in the house—no one had lighted the fireplace—and he shivered slightly and rubbed his hands together, the whole act unconscious, his thoughts on other things. He crossed the hall and went into the kitchen, wanting something warm now, a cup of coffee. But the kitchen range was cold and the coffeepot empty.

He stood there with his hands thrust deep into his pockets, his mind too numb to think beyond the moment.

He heard Virginia's door close and heard her come down the stairs. He moved to the kitchen doorway and waited for her.

Virginia paused at the foot of the staircase, startled — she had not heard her father come home.

He stared at her for a long moment, a haggard, red-eyed man punished by his thoughts — by a guilt that had been riding him like a yoke.

She said uneasily: "I didn't know you were home."

He shrugged and moved toward her. He saw now that she was dressed to go out, and anger stirred in him.

"Where are you going?"

She recoiled from the hostility in his voice. She said without force: "I'm going out."

"At this hour? Alone?" Frank's voice was rough.

She stood silent before him, momentarily cowed; she had little defense against him.

Frank shook his head like a man trying to clear his

brain of cobwebs.

"Isn't it enough your brother's out there," he said harshly, "asking to get himself killed? And for what? My God — for what?"

Virginia stood stiffly by the staircase post, her eyes searching her father's haggard face. There was sorrow in her, but she had no tongue to express it.

He was stung by her muteness. "Damn it!" he snarled. "Don't you ever have anything to say?"

She stood still, unable to move past his wrath, but determined not to go back to her room.

"He wouldn't listen to me," Frank said bitterly. "He wouldn't even talk to me!" He turned away from her, his eyes tortured. "I don't know your brother any more; I can't reach him!"

His hands clenched as though trying to grasp at something elusive. He was a big man who had gotten his way most of his life; he was helpless now, and it was destroying him.

"What's happened to him?" he flung at her. "Why is Roger like this?"

Virginia's voice was low; she looked down at the

floor. "Don't you know?"

"Know what?"

She hung her head, unable to answer. He jerked her chin up, his eyes burning into hers. "Look at me!"

She shrank away from the look in his eyes. She tried to go past him to the door, but he grabbed her and flung her roughly against the wall, his dark anxiety finding an outlet in lashing out at her.

"If it hadn't been for you" he grated, "getting mixed up with that Anders whelp—" He sucked in a harsh breath. "With a dozen boys in this town to chose from, in heaven's name, *why him?"*

She stared at him now, her face a bleak and bitter mask.

"A dozen boys, Father?"

Her right hand went up to her face, her fingers probing lightly.

"Look at me, Pa!" For once her voice was firm, almost harsh. "For once, just once — *look at me!"*

He stared at her, angry, not comprehending.

"What's wrong with you?"

The spark of defiance faded in her. "You," she said,

her voice dying. "You and Roger. *He* filled your life, Pa. Not me. Not even Mother."

Frank frowned, groping his way through her words for their meaning. "He's a boy," he defended himself. "A man grows close to his son."

She nodded stiffly, her eyes misting.

"But not to his daughter?"

Frank's face darkened. "Are you trying to tell me that's why you took up with the Anders boy?"

Virginia's head came up, her eyes meeting his.

"Billy needed me." There was an ache in her voice. "No one here needed me, not even after Mother died."

He looked at her, the anger and the anxiety fading in him. He stared at the frail, not pretty girl he had sired, seeing her clearly as if for the first time — seeing what he had done to her, and appalled at the knowledge.

"Virginia, I'm sorry. I didn't know."

She turned away from him as he fumbled with words that no longer mattered, with emotions that were being shown too late. He stepped in front of her again, not with authority, but irresolutely now, feeling only that he should stop her, somehow make up to her for the lost and irreversible years.

"Where, Virginia — where are you going?"

"To stop Roger — if I can." There was a sad and lonely sound in her voice. "To do what I should have done hours ago."

She pushed past him, and Frank stood there, arms by his side, unable to stop her . . . .

— XIX —
"I KILLED CYNTHIA CHOQUETTE!"

The group of men waited in front of the Mason Freight Line warehouse, rifles held tensely, faces closed in anger. A carriage, teamless, its poles resting on the ground, waited by the warehouse loading platform.

The door opened, and two men stepped out onto the platform. Roger Mason had a length of fuse looped around his arm. Hank carried a small keg in his arms.

Roger looked down at the waiting men. "Fifty pounds of gunpowder!" he said. There was venom in his voice. "They'll go — one way or another!"

Moving quickly up the street, keeping to the shadows, Brannigan turned toward the Mason house. It was quiet in Brassada Hill now; even the angry voices that had come from the Longhorn Bar were stilled.

In the pale moonlight, the Mason house loomed large, its gables casting shadows. Brannigan crossed to the door and knocked, a grim-faced man knowing that time was running out on him and that he had to get his answers now — and fast.

He was about to knock again when the door jerked open. Frank Mason stood framed in the light from the hallway. He stared angrily at the lawman, then started to shut the door on him.

Brannigan shouldered his way inside.

Frank turned to face him, his hands balled at his sides.

"Get out of here!" he said thickly.

Brannigan ignored him. He walked to the archway and glanced into the sitting room; then he swung back to Frank, his voice grim.

"Where's your daughter?"

"What do you want of her?" Frank moved toward

him, his eyes bitter. "What are you after?"

"The truth," Brannigan said. "It might save a lot of killing!"

"If there's killing tonight, it'll be your doing, Brannigan! *Your* doing!"

His hands dropped away as he turned from the marshal. "If you had only let Billy Anders lie —"

Brannigan's voice cut flatly across his. "Billy didn't kill Cynthia Choquette!"

Mason turned slowly. The anger drained out of him, leaving him a hollow man, staring.

Brannigan said: "I found this in her trunk." He held out the ribbon-tied roll of paper.

"You know what it is, don't you, Mr. Mason? Your name's on it —"

Mason's voice was stiff, empty. "You had no right —"

Brannigan's voice rode over his. "It's a marriage certificate, made out in Louisiana twenty-three years ago, the day Cynthia Choquette became Mrs. Frank Mason!"

Frank Mason stared at the wall, his world closing

down on him.

"You did marry her?"

Frank nodded slowly. "To have and to hold," he said. There was no life in his voice, no feeling. "To have and to hold until death do us part . . . ."

He turned to face Brannigan. "But I held her only long enough for her to bear a son; then she left us." He was silent for a moment. "I thought she was dead—until the day she showed up here in Brassada Hill to blackmail me, to destroy me."

His eyes met Brannigan's. "I don't know why, Marshal. I don't know what she had against me. But I didn't kill her."

He turned and walked slowly into the living room and sank down into a chair. "I didn't kill her," he repeated. "But so help me, I'm glad she's dead!" He put his face in his hands, his words muffled now. "I'm glad she's dead."

The sky was clearing over Brassada Hill. But a sense of impending violence hung like a thickening fog over the empty streets.

Joe Sequoia and Jim Granite waited inside the mortuary. The passing hours had put a strain on them; they looked grimmer, harsher.

Joe turned to look as the wall clock struck eleven.

"Hour of the dog," Jim said. He was still in the chair tilted back against the wall, but the lightness in his tone had an edge. "Chinese time, Joe."

Joe went to the window and looked out.

"Quiet out there," he commented. "Too quiet."

Jim tipped his chair to the floor and got to his feet, shifting his rifle easily to his left hand.

"Someone ought to check on Jud. He's been gone a long time —"

Joe suddenly lifted a warning hand, waving for silence. Both men listened for a moment; then Jim stepped silently to the bolted door, and Joe drew his Colt, covering him.

The light footsteps outside stopped at the door. Jim eased the bolt back, then yanked the door open, bringing his rifle up as he did so.

Virginia Mason shrank back, the shock of surprise in her eyes. Jim glanced past her into the dark street.

She seemed to be alone.

"Looking for someone, miss?"

Virginia pushed past him into the office. Jim frowned; he closed the door, bolted it, then turned to look at her. Joe slowly holstered his gun.

Jim's voice was cold. "What do you want?"

Virginia eyed the two unshaven men. "Marshal Brannigan," she answered. Her voice was small, tight. "I'm Virginia Mason."

Joe said: "He's not here."

Virginia cast a quick glance around the office. She was wound up tight. She had come there to talk to Brannigan. Now she looked at the two lawmen, uncertain what to do.

"You come to join the wake, Miss Mason?" Jim's voice was backed by a crooked grin.

"I must see Marshal Brannigan!" Virginia blurted. "Why?"

Virginia looked at Jim, at Joe. Her face was pinched with helpless uncertainty.

Jim moved toward her. *"Why,* Miss Mason?"

She turned away from him, moving toward the

door. There was panic in her eyes. She wanted Brannigan, not these men she didn't know. But Jim grabbed her by the arm, swinging her around to face him.

"What do you want to tell Marshal Brannigan?"

Virginia's breath went out in a soft and bitter sigh. "I killed Cynthia Choquette!"

The two men eyed her in a cold and wondering silence.

"I killed her," Virginia repeated, but there was peace in her now, at last. "Billy Anders took the blame for me!"

Jim swung around to Joe, his voice hard. "Find Jud —"

The tearing smash of a rifle bullet through the boarded window interrupted him. It ripped into the face of the wall clock, stilling it.

Jim moved instinctively. He pulled Virginia to the floor with him as Joe crouched, drawing his gun.

Roger's voice came loudly after the echoes of the shot had faded.

"You've got five minutes, Brannigan! Come out

and take Billy's body with you!"

The two lawmen stared at each other, then turned to look at Virginia Mason, who was backing off, straightening against the wall. Her face was white as she stared at the door . . . .

— XX —
THE BITTER TRUTH

Roger Mason waited in the shadows of the black-smith's shop, a rifle in his hands. The others were behind him and scattered along the walk, all armed. They were waiting for an answer from Sam Hill's place.

"You hear me, Brannigan?" Roger stepped out of the shadows, standing boldly on the walk now, a wild look in his eyes. He fired a shot through the boarded window, and a moment later the light inside the mortuary went out. The building now stood dark and silent across the street.

"Damn you, Brannigan!" Roger yelled. "You can't

get away! The back door's covered!"

There was no answer from inside the mortuary.

Roger turned to the man by his side. "All right," he said bitterly. "Tell them to roll her out!"

The man went to the alley and made a motion. Wheels creaked faintly as the carriage was rolled out into the street, its poles up, lashed to the carriage sides. It rolled easily through the mud, stopping in the middle of the street, pointed at the mortuary.

"Come on out, Brannigan!"

The front of Sam Hill's undertaking parlors remained strangely quiet.

Roger turned to the two men who had pushed the carriage out of the alley. "All right, Hank —"

The keg of gunpowder sat in the small bed behind the carriage's high seat. The length of fuse trailed from it. Hank nodded, struck a match on the tail-gate, lighted the fuse and watched it sputter.

Roger yelled: "We gave you a chance, Brannigan! Now we're going to blow you out!"

He joined Hank and the other man behind the carriage. Together they began to push it toward the mortuary . . . .

Joe Sequoia was peering through a crack in the boarded window, his gun cocked and ready. Jim was standing by the door, ignoring the girl, who was frozen, staring in horror . . . .

Jim said harshly: "What are they up to, Joe?"

Joe's eyes narrowed, and he licked his lips. "They've got a carriage out there. They're rolling it this way —"

Jim frowned. "Blow us out?" Then, as it hit him: "The crazy fools!"

He jerked the bolt back and yanked the door open. He started out, his rifle held down by his side.

A rifle from across the street blasted at him. He fell back, dropping his weapon, and tried to twist away from the door as Roger yelled: "That you, Branni-gan?" There was a savage glee in his voice.

A strangled cry broke out of Virginia. "Roger—no! My God—no!"

She evaded Joe's instinctive reach for her and ran out the door. Joe turned to Granite and dragged him away from the open door toward the side wall . . .

Roger Mason swung his rifle to target the running girl and almost pulled the trigger before Hank grabbed his arm and said harshly: "It's your sister!"

He waited then, his face shocked, as the girl came toward him, stumbling in the mud, her voice thin, close to hysteria.

"Roger—no—no—"

The carriage was stalled in the middle of the street; the fuse was burning quickly toward its end point in the powder keg.

Roger and Hank stood frozen, unaware . . . .

Virginia reached the carriage, pushed Roger aside and leaned over the tail-gate, tearing the sizzling fuse free, flinging it away . . . .

Roger came to life then. He shoved her roughly away from the carriage. She staggered and fell in the mud.

"Go home!" he yelled at her. "Get away from here!"

She dragged herself to her feet, staggered toward

her brother and grabbed his rifle arm. "It's all wrong, Roger—all—wrong—"

He pushed her away, past listening to anything now. He turned his rifle on Hank as men watched in frozen silence from the blacksmith's shop.

"Roll it, Hank!"

Hank and the man with him put their shoulders to the tail-gate. They rolled the carriage up to the mortuary door, ducking as a shot blasted at them from inside. Then they ran back across the slippery, muddy street to join the men in the shadows on the walk.

Roger raised his rifle. He was protected from the men inside by the carriage, and he drew a bead on the gunpowder keg.

"Your last chance, Brannigan!"

Virginia stood in front of him, a bedraggled, defiant figure. "Listen to me, Roger. Marshal Brannigan was right! Billy didn't kill Cynthia Choquette."

He ignored her. "Come on out, Brannigan —"

"I killed her!" Virginia cried. "Don't you understand? *I killed your mother, Roger!*"

Roger froze, his face twisted into a terrible mask.

Pain, shame and disbelief ground it into a gargoyle mixture.

"No," he said. It was a low, terrible sound, forced out of him. *"No!"*

"I killed her!" Virginia repeated. "It was an accident. She tried to hurt me. She had the shotgun. I grabbed at it, and it went off."

She took a step toward her brother, standing there, his rifle gripped in his hands. She saw the look on his face, and there was an ache in her heart.

"Don't you see, Roger—don't you see?" A sob broke from her lips. "It was all for nothing—the beating you took from Billy. Because he told you the truth that day—the truth we've tried to hide from you —"

Roger's voice was an animal cry of pain, of defiance. "No! You're lying! You're trying to cover up for Billy! My mother's there, in the cemetery —"

"I'm not lying," Virginia said. Tears were trickling down her cheeks. "She told me, Roger—she told who she was, why she had come here to Brassada Hill. She was going to tell you herself. She wanted to hurt you, as she was hurting Father."

Roger spun away from her. He didn't want to believe this — *he couldn't believe it!* Cynthia
Choquette, the town madam, *his mother?*

He blotted it out of his mind. He turned to the mortuary where Joe and Granite waited and brought his
rifle up to target the powder keg.

"Brannigan, you put her up to this! You've got her
lying for you!"

His voice rang wildly along the silent street. "Come
out, damn you, or I'll put a bullet in that powder keg
and blow you out of Brassada Hill!"

"Roger!" The sharp, cold voice came from behind
Mason. "I'm over here, Roger!"

Roger turned, his eyes glaring at the man coming
toward him in the street. Far behind, his father was a
shadowy stumbling figure, following.

Brannigan paused some twenty feet away. "She's
telling you the truth, Roger. Billy didn't kill your
mother —"

Roger stared at him. He saw only a man who had
thwarted him from the beginning, a man who had
stubbornly torn his world apart because he had prom-

ised Billy Anders a burial in Brassada Hill . . . .

"The truth, Brannigan?" His voice was shrill. "This is the truth."

He jerked his rifle muzzle up, fired, and was levering for another shot when Brannigan's bullet hit him, sending him sprawling backward into the mud . . . .

Virginia took a few steps toward her brother, then stopped, her hands coming up to cover her face. She began to cry silently, bitterly.

Joe Sequoia came out to the walk, his rifle held ready. Brannigan shot him a look.

"Where's Jim?"

"Inside." Joe's voice was easy. "He was hit — not bad."

Brannigan walked slowly to Roger and hunkered down beside him. He pulled Roger's coat aside and eyed the bullet hole in his chest.

Frank Mason's boots made sucking sounds as he came up behind the marshal.

Brannigan looked up at him. "He'll live." He straightened and slipped his Colt back into its holster. The men in front of the blacksmith's shop were silent, all anger drained from them.

"You should have told him," Brannigan said. His voice was toneless. "It didn't have to come to this."

"Told him?" Frank's eyes were bitter as he stared down at his son. "What do you tell a boy about his mother? A woman like her? What do you tell him, Marshal?"

The Brassada Hill cemetery stood on a small knoll a mile from town. It was a fair day, the sun shining in a cloudless sky. The mugginess had gone with the storm, and there was a freshness in the air.

Virginia and her father stood on one side of Billy's grave; Brannigan and Joe Sequoia on the other. Jim Granite waited by the cemetery gate, his left arm in a sling. He was mounted, holding the reins of two horses.

The gravediggers had finished and were moving away. No one else had come out to the cemetery. It would take a long time for Brassada Hill to come to terms with this.

Billy's grave lay next to that of Cynthia Choquette. Just beyond lay Frank's wife, the woman he had married after Cynthia Choquette had deserted him. He had married her in good faith, and the fact that legally she was not his wife was meaningless now.

A small headboard marked Billy's grave, as one marked Cynthia's; there were some flowers on both.

This was what Billy Anders had wanted, Brannigan thought. For good or bad, he belonged there!

Frank Mason raised his eyes to Brannigan. "I'll wire a full explanation to the governor," he said. "I'll see that you are not held accountable."

Brannigan's voice was dry. "Thanks."

He walked out with Joe Sequoia, and each man mounted beside Jim Granite.

Jim was looking off toward the two figures by the grave of Billy Anders.

"Reckon there's some good in everyone," he said, "even in a boy like Billy Anders."

Brannigan nodded, his voice short. "Yeah."

He swung away from the cemetery, the other two

falling in beside him. They rode away from Brassada Hill, and they didn't look back.

THE END